Kikko climbed up behind the abomination. *This is going to be fun.*

Then it got dark.

It's morning. It can't get dark. And it's not cloudy.

Realizing he was now in something's shadow, he turned around.

The sky was blotted out by a ten-foot-long head with two horns on top of it.

Whoa. The big daddy of all abominations.

Kikko screamed.

The head leaned forward. Its teeth were numerous, looked to be razor-sharp, and were heading straight for Kikko.

GARGANTUA

A Novel by

K. ROBERT ANDREASSI

Based on the Teleplay by

RONALD PARKER

TOR®

A TOM DOHERTY ASSOCIATES BOOK
NEW YORK

This is a work of fiction. All the characters and events portrayed in this book are either products of the author's imagination or are used fictitiously.

GARGANTUA

A Tor Book
Published by Tom Doherty Associates, Inc.
175 Fifth Avenue
New York, NY 10010

Tor Books on the World Wide Web:
http://www.tor.com

Tor® is a registered trademark of Tom Doherty Associates, Inc.

ISBN: 0-812-57098-7

First edition: May 1998

Printed in the United States of America

0 9 8 7 6 5 4 3 2 1

For the Geek Patrol—Drewshi, the Hawk-Man, the Lip-Chick, and the Tall Cool One— for all those Wednesday nights.

ACKNOWLEDGMENTS

I would like to thank Ronald Parker, the writer and producer of *Gargantua*, who went above and beyond the call of duty to help me flesh out his script; Tor Books editor Greg Cox for giving me the assignment in the first place and for generally being a good egg; Greg's noble assistant Karla Zounek for keeping me up to date; Ms. G. A. DeCandido for invaluable editorial input; Marina Frants, for local color, scuba diving and fish neepery, and general support; *Ocean Realm* magazine, especially the various articles in their Winter 1997/98 issue; Jim Macdonald for invaluable technical expertise; Spiff's Newt & Salamander web page, which has everything you ever wanted to know about salamanders but were afraid to ask (http://www.users.interport.net/~spiff/Newt&Salamander.html); and Key West musician Michael McCloud and the sadly now-defunct Seattle trio Uncle Bonsai for musical inspiration.

PROLOGUE

"'mon, 'Stairway to Heaven' is the best rock and roll song *ever*."

As always, John made that pronouncement at the loudest possible volume. Marina sighed. She'd known John since high school, and he always seemed to subscribe to the theory that whoever spoke loudest had to be right.

Dave, of course, chimed in. He was constitutionally incapable of agreeing with anything John said—not difficult, really, but it was a knee-jerk reaction. "Please. The song sucks. Hell, Robert Plant wrote the goddamn thing, and he doesn't even have any idea what it means."

John was in the middle of sipping from his beer bottle, and so couldn't reply verbally without spilling it.

That left it to John's fiancée to come to his defense. "What difference does that make?" Laura asked. "I mean, all those stupid Bob Dylan songs you drool over don't make a lot of sense, either."

"Look," John said, having finished his sip and now

screwing the bottle down into the sand, "every time radio stations do those best rock songs of all time polls, 'Stairway to Heaven' *always* wins. Period, end of sentence."

John also liked to say *period, end of sentence* as if it would actually end the argument. It never did, but he always looked disappointed when someone kept the discussion going anyhow.

Marina turned and gazed out into the ocean as she scrunched sand between her bare toes. The sun had started to set, painting the sky in glorious bursts of red, orange, and purple. *So of course the guys are talking about music*, she thought with an internal sigh. *We travel halfway 'round the world for sun, surf, and scuba diving, and they sit here and have the same stupid conversations they have back home.*

Marina and her friends sat in a circle on Malau's largest beach. A bonfire blazed in the circle's center, and Marina's boyfriend Greg was holding a large pan over it by its long handle. Inside the pan was the first batch of fish that the others had caught that day while Marina, Greg, and Dave went diving. The group had decided to escape the latest in a series of brutal Minneapolis winters by taking a tropical vacation in the South Seas. Malau— one of the few local islands whose economy relied more on fishing than tourism—proved the best choice, as they wanted to avoid the usual tourist traps.

Greg got into the act now: "What about 'Layla'?"

John got his disappointed look. "That isn't a song, it's two separate songs that have nothing to do with each other."

Marina sighed again. She had been hoping that her boyfriend would stay out of it, but no such luck.

"Yeah, but 'Layla' has the hook—the guitar riff. I mean, *everybody* knows that guitar riff. Name me *one* riff from 'Stairway to Heaven'."

Marina suddenly stood up. "Guys, I'm gonna take a walk, okay?"

Various murmurs of "yeah," "okay," and "whatever" came from the group. Greg said, "The first batch of fish is almost ready, hon."

"I'm not really hungry," Marina said, which was a lie. She just hated eating newly captured fish. She knew it wasn't rational—back home, she would gleefully sink her teeth into fried shrimp or smoked salmon—but here, in a place where fish were primarily a subject for her underwater photography, eating them seemed wrong somehow.

Carol also rose. "I'll go with you," she said.

At first Marina was going to object, but then she nodded. She didn't really know Carol very well. Marina had been friends with the others since either high school or college, but Carol was just the girlfriend Dave happened to have on this particular trip. He went through about four a year, and indeed had been dating a woman named Kim when they first planned the trip. *But hey, maybe this'll give me the chance to get to know her better,* Marina thought.

She looked out again at the colors of the sky. The purple was starting to overtake the red and orange. *Besides, I have to share this sunset with* someone.

They started to walk down the beach quietly at first. A warm breeze wafted gently through Marina's hair as she watched the colorburst that was the South Seas sky. Sometimes she wondered why she stayed in so cold and bitter a place as Minneapolis when places like this existed. Right now, she felt like she would have been content to spend her entire life just sitting with her eyes closed and letting this amazing breeze caress her face.

This place is magic, she thought, not for the first time. At sunset, the sky had more colors than a Monet painting. At night, the stars came out in numbers she never would have believed possible growing up as a city girl. And during the day, the water was a deep, pure blue.

"Marina?" Carol asked, startling her—she had temporarily forgotten the other woman's presence.

"Yeah?"

"Do you have *any* idea what they're talking about?"

Marina couldn't help laughing, as she forced herself back to the real world. "Music—rock and roll songs."

"Oh, okay."

Marina stared at her companion in something like shock. "You date Dave and you don't listen to rock and roll?"

Carol shrugged and folded her arms in order to rub them. Marina noticed goosebumps on the other woman's arms, which surprised her—while it was cooler than the one hundred degrees it had been that afternoon, it was still quite warm out.

"He tried to get me to listen to some stuff, but— I dunno, it's just noise, y'know?" Carol's voice suddenly grew distant. "That is *so* beautiful."

"Yeah, I don't think I'm ever going to get tired of the sunsets here."

"Hm? Oh, I meant the music those guys are playing over there. *That's* real music, y'know?"

Marina blinked. She had noticed the music playing, of course—the drums sometimes threatened to drown out everyone except John—but hadn't paid it much heed. About thirty feet from where she and her friends had set up their bonfire, a bunch of locals had gotten together for a kind of jam session—in fact, their playing was what prompted the discussion of which rock and roll song was the greatest in the first place. Marina had the tinnest of tin ears, and so had no idea what kind of music they played, nor whether it was any good. It was heavy on percussion, a steady, rhythmic, loud beat. Certainly the people dancing to the music seemed to think it was worth bopping around to. They all had huge smiles on their faces. Marina couldn't help but compare them to the people dancing at her uncle's wedding the previous summer; they had smiled, too, but they were the plastered-on smiles of the terminally-polite-but-not-really-caring-that-much. These people were genuinely enjoying themselves, as enchanted by the music they danced to as Marina was by the setting she walked in. *But then, that could just be the native spirit of happiness.*

Good God, she thought, aghast, *listen to me—I sound like some kind of British colonel in a pith helmet travelling to the dark continent for the first time.* But it was hard not to think of the Malauans as anything but congenial and happy with life. The unconditional friendliness with which the locals treated everyone—even a bunch of loud, obnoxious tourists from Minnesota—truly delighted Marina, and just added to the magic.

Suddenly, her knees felt like they were shivering—but she still wasn't in the least bit cold. Then the tremor became more pronounced and a rumbling sound seemed to come from all around her. *Great, another stupid tremor.* The brochure had promised "at worst" the occasional tremor, and the travel agent insisted that the island had "maybe one a week," but there had been at least one per day since their arrival four days earlier. It was the one thing that spoiled the magic.

The tremor died down after about ten seconds, followed by the sounds of whooping, cheering, and hollering from the gang around the bonfire—John was loudest, of course. Marina shook her head.

"They're nuts," Carol said. "This whole island could crack down the middle, and they'd think it was some kind of roller coaster ride."

"Well, y'know, we are here to have fun," Marina said, surprised to find herself coming to the others' defense when, in fact, she agreed with what Carol was saying. *I guess it's that instinct to protect the herd against out-siders*, she thought with a small smile.

"Not everything is necessarily fun. I mean, Dave keeps going off and diving with you guys even though I don't dive."

"You can get certified here, y'know."

Carol shook her head vigorously. "You don't under-stand, I'm claustrophobic. I can't even go snorkeling."

"Oh."

"I just wish he'd show some consideration, y'know? I mean, you've known him a while—is he always like this?"

Dammit, Dave, Marina thought toward her friend, *you're doing it again.* Every single girlfriend of his got to the point where they'd ask one of his friends if he was "always like this," and she was sick and tired of it. She especially didn't want to have to deal with it on her vaca-tion when there was a perfectly good sunset to bask in. *I guess it isn't just the tremors that can spoil the magic.*

"Don't you think you ought to be talking to Dave about this?"

"I tried—he just blows me off, says, 'We're on vaca-tion, don't be a pain.' "

Well, he's got a point, Marina almost said aloud but restrained herself.

Then something caught the corner of her eye. "Hey, look at that!"

"What?"

She bent down to pick up a seashell that almost glowed in the dusky light. In the usual concave shape of shells, the inside was coral pink, but the outer part seemed alive with color, a combination of pinks, purples, whites, and grays.

"Here's another one," Carol said, picking up one that was more of a solid pink.

Marina smiled. *Good, that distracted her.*

They spent the next minute or so gathering up shells. They'd probably abandon them before they went back to the small bungalow the group had rented, but it was a fun little diversion.

"What's all that?" Carol asked.

Marina followed her gaze to a tide pool that was covered in netting secured by buoys. She had a feeling that she knew what those nets were for. *But what the hell, let's explore it anyhow. Anything to keep Carol's mind off Dave.*

As they got closer, wading into the pool up to their ankles, her suspicions proved correct: it was fishing net. "Oh look," she said, a note of distaste in her voice, as she picked up a small lobster. Next to her, Carol liberated a large prawn.

Then she felt something tug at her feet. At first she thought it was seaweed, but then it dug sharply into her ankles.

Another tug, and this time, she almost stumbled face-first into the shallow water. Something was yanking the netting around.

Carol said, "Something's trapped down there."

Dropping both the lobster and her seashells, Marina started to clamber out of the tide pool, Carol doing likewise.

Yet another tug—more of a violent thrash, really—and this time, Marina *did* fall face-first into the water. Instinctively, she held her breath and closed her eyes before her face struck the water, feeling like someone had hit her with a damp washcloth.

The net continued to yank at her ankle with ever harder tugs. Marina tried to get up, but couldn't get her legs to cooperate. Falling down had only entangled them in the net more.

A gurgling noise sounded next to her: Carol, trying to scream, but she too was face-down in the water. Marina struggled more, but only found herself tangled up worse. *I'd kill for my dive knife right now*, she thought.

The yanking was steadier now, dragging Marina and Carol into the ocean. Carol had managed to turn herself over and was crying out with a full-throated scream, uninhibited by salt water.

Marina found herself remembering a conversation with Dave the day they arrived. "Where are the lifeguards?" she had asked.

"We're not back home," Dave had said. "Everything isn't regulated up the kazoo and people don't litigate at the drop of a hat."

At the time, Marina had found that refreshing. People had to get by on their own. Self-reliance. Marina had always prided herself on being self-reliant.

Now, she cursed whatever idiot thought that the beaches of Malau didn't require lifeguards. *Self-reliance doesn't do me a lot of good when I'm tangled in a net!*

She had stopped struggling, as it only made things worse, and tried to relax, hoping that it might loosen the net enough for her to swim out. Sadly, Carol did not come to the same realization, and she continued to thrash about more and more as they were dragged out of the tide pool and into the ocean proper.

Marina remembered that Carol said something about being claustrophobic.

Then she saw it.

At first she thought it was a mask of some kind, floating in the ocean. Even in Malau, one always found such detritus in the water, and it was exactly the sort of thing that might get caught in a fishing net.

But masks didn't blink.

They didn't try to forcibly remove themselves from nets, either.

It's a head, she realized as the thing yanked itself sud-

denly to the left in an apparent attempt to free itself. The
thing was green and scaly, with a small horn protruding
from just above the eyes, like some kind of lizard or
gecko or salamander or something—amphibians weren't
Marina's strong suit.

"Ow!" she cried as the net started digging into her
flesh. As good an idea as it might have been to try to relax
herself, it was doomed to fail when two other bodies in
the net—Carol and this lizard-thing—were thrashing
around like they were having seizures.

The head shot upward, and Marina got a quick look at
the thing's long neck before the net twisted and yanked
free of its moorings in the tide pool. Marina found herself
suddenly completely underwater.

She hadn't had a chance to hold her breath this time,
and she gagged as salt water filled her nose and mouth.
The net pulled inexorably tighter around her legs, chest,
and neck.

Marina had managed to keep a relatively clear head,
but now she couldn't breathe and was effectively bound.
Panic overtook her, and she too started thrashing about,
trying to get a grip on the net to pull it off, trying to move
toward the surface, trying to scream, trying to do *anything*, but to just *get out of this*.

Her eye caught sight of something else in the net—it
had to be the body that went with the head she saw. The
forelegs were pretty strange-looking—more like claws.
Plus, the body was as big as she was. And it seemed to be
growing black spots.

Marina realized that the spots weren't on the lizard,
they were dancing in front of her eyes—she was blacking
out.

One of the leg/claws ripped through the net, and the
cords tightened around Marina's neck.

She tried to scream.

Then everything went black.

■ ■ ■

"Did you see that?"

"What?"

"Thought I saw something move in the water."

"It's the ocean, Greg, things move in it all the time. It's called an ecosystem."

"Hardy-har-har. The fish is just about done."

"Haven't Carol and Marina gotten back yet?"

"Nah, Marina's probably drooling over the sunset or something. We won't see them for ages."

"Hey, what about 'Born to Run'?"

ONE

Brandon Ellway stared at the two suitcases, one garment bag, and three duffel bags in the room he and his father were to share during their stay in Malau, trying to figure out which one to unpack first.

Dad had told Brandon to unpack the luggage and check the two laptops while he went off to supervise the delivery of his specialized equipment. Dad always did that—no matter where they went, he always stood over the people who delivered all his toys to the hotel room.

Malau had just been the latest stop; Brandon and his father had been on the road for months, travelling to all sorts of interesting places, stopping home only long enough to restock on things like clothes.

Deciding to get the unpleasantness overwith, Brandon opened up his father's suitcase. It was, naturally, a disaster area—clothes strewn about, unfolded and disorganized. As usual, Dad just threw stuff into the suitcase without thinking. At least he hadn't mixed the dirty laundry up with the clean clothes, but that was only because Brandon himself had made sure the laundry was done their last day in Vancouver.

Sighing, Brandon sorted through Dad's clothes, folded them, and put them away. Their room had two dressers with three drawers each. The underwear and socks went in the top drawer, shirts in the second, pants and shorts in the third. Then he hung up the garment bag, which contained Dad's two suits, in the room's closet.

That left his own suitcase, which was meticulously organized, just the way Mom had taught him.

Mom.

It had been a year since Brandon's mother's death. But the twelve-year-old refused to dwell on it. He wasn't a dumb kid anymore; he wasn't going to let it get to him. After all, he was Dad's assistant—or *intern*, as he called it, but Brandon liked the other word better.

Even before Mom died, Brandon had been helping out. What was it that guy from that magazine called them? "One big happy science family." Brandon probably knew enough about marine biology at twelve to qualify for a Bachelor's Degree in the subject.

He finished putting away his own clothes, as well as his prize possession: the acid-free box that contained his precious *Captain Marvel* comics. These were the old Fawcett comics from the 1940s that C. C. Beck and Otto Binder did before the publishers of *Superman* sued them for infringing on their copyright. Brandon had inherited the comics from his grandfather, and he absolutely loved them. He refused to leave them anywhere; despite the risks, he always had to have the comics with him wherever he went.

He stowed the comics in the closet, then turned to the two laptops. One was Dad's, used to construct models, fill in charts, and make notes. The other was Brandon's, used partly to compile various bits of data that Dad needed, partly to play games (Brandon especially enjoyed a logic game he'd acquired off the Internet), but primarily for his home schooling.

Home schooling. Yeah, right. Like I've got a home. Sure, they technically lived in San Diego, but it wasn't like Brandon ever spent any time there anymore. Home were these two suitcases, Dad's all messy and disorganized, Brandon's neat and pristine, just like Mom's always was.

Stop thinking about her. You're over it, remember?

Brandon unzipped the case for Dad's laptop and put it on the desk. As he set it down, he heard a soft clunk from inside one of the flaps. He ripped open the velcro to find a picture frame.

Mom.

It was the picture of her that Dad had taken on that boat in Key West—what turned out to be their last trip before Mom was diagnosed with the brain tumor. Brandon hadn't liked Key West all that much, but the boat trip was fun. Mom looked really cool with the wind blowing her hair all around—kind of like a fashion model, almost.

I'm not gonna cry. I'm a big kid. Big kids don't cry.

He'd been good. He hadn't thought about Mom in weeks. Not even the last time he unpacked. But that stupid bellhop was talking to that other stupid bellhop about those two people that died on the beach last night, and that reminded Brandon of when Dad first told him about Mom, and—

Stop thinking about it!

He booted up Dad's laptop, then set the picture down next to the bed closest to the door. That was going to be Dad's bed, since Brandon preferred to sleep near the window, and Dad always let him. Then he unloaded his own laptop and booted it up.

While he waited for them to go through their startup routines, Brandon looked out the window. Though given the highfalutin' name of the Hotel Ritz, their lodgings were, in fact, in a fairly ramshackle one-story wooden building that made the average Motel 6 back home look like the Plaza. Brandon's first thought upon seeing it was that they were reliving the youth of Abraham Lincoln in his log cabin.

Still, they did have a view of the beach where, according to Dad, they'd probably do most of their work. Unlike the beaches back home in San Diego, this place was gorgeous. In all the time he'd been helping his parents out, Brandon had never seen water quite this blue before. *Unspoiled* was the word Dad had used, and from the way he described it, Brandon was worried that this island would be full of natives in grass skirts who used barter for trade.

Based on what he'd seen so far, this wasn't the case. Even this rinky-dink hotel had air conditioning, everyone spoke better English than Brandon did, and there wasn't a grass skirt in sight.

A yawn crept up on him, then seemed to wash over his entire body as his mouth opened wide and he stretched his arms out. *This place may be nice, but it sure is far away from everywhere else.* The flight had taken hours, and with all the switching around and the dinky planes they had to take on the last leg of the trip, it felt like it took longer to fly from Manila to Malau than it did the much longer distance from Vancouver to Manila. Brandon had slept as much as he could on the various flights, but he still wanted some time to relax, maybe take a nap. *Hope Dad feels the same.*

A clicking noise brought Brandon's attention away from the splendid view and to the door, through which walked his father.

Weirdly, Dad came in alone.

"Where's all the stuff, Dad?"

Dad smiled. "The 'stuff' is out on the beach, which is

where we're gonna be in a few minutes. How're Jack and Jill doing?"

Brandon rolled his eyes. He never understood why Dad had to name the computers, and always after some kind of duo. The previous two laptops, before they upgraded to the latest notebooks, were called Thelma and Louise.

In answer to Dad's question, he said, "They're booting up now. But we're all unpacked and everything. Do we have to go out to the beach right away?"

Dad nodded. " 'Fraid so."

"Can't you start without me?" Brandon asked, thinking once more of naps.

Putting his hand to his chest, Dad got all sarcastic. "What? Start without my loyal intern?"

"Assistant."

"Fine, assistant. Either way, you know I need you down there." He smiled. "C'mon, finish up with the machines, then put on your bathing suit."

Brandon frowned. "Bathing suit?"

Dad laughed as he unbuttoned his shirt. "Or shorts, I don't care. But we're on a tropical island now. We go out like this, we'll suffocate."

Brandon looked down at his own outfit: a long-sleeved Polo shirt and jeans. Fine for Vancouver, but not so much for here. "Yeah, okay," he said, pulling the Polo shirt over his head, then moving over to the dresser to pull out a T-shirt and a pair of shorts.

After both Brandon and his father had changed, the boy checked out the laptops. "Everything looks cool, Dad. No error messages or viruses or anything. Want me to run the applications?"

"Nah. And don't bother bringing them down—don't wanna get sand in 'em. We're just doing the basic stuff today, water temperature and the like. So bring a paper notebook."

Brandon nodded and grabbed a legal pad and pen from one of the duffels. "Let's go to work, Dad."

"Look, Kal, it's *my* front page. All you gotta do is print it….No, I didn't clear it with Manny, why the hell should I?…Look, Manny believes in freedom of the press just like me, so…c'mon, Kal, it's not like this is a big secret or anything, especially the way that John Dovrojer guy is carrying on at the top of his lungs….Kal, this ain't a discussion, all right? It's my paper, and I'm tellin' you that that picture of those two girls is goin' on the front page….All right, then….'bye."

Paul Bateman sighed as he hung up the phone. Kal had never given him this kind of hard time before. But then, Paul had never printed the story of two tourist corpses on his front page before, either.

Prior to Paul setting up the *Malau Weekly News*, Kal's clientele at his print shop had consisted primarily of signs, pamphlets, and booklets—barely enough for him to stay in business. He also used equipment that was top of the line when he got it in 1978. The revenue from printing a weekly paper allowed him to upgrade—to Paul's extreme gratitude, since his journalism training at the University of California at Berkeley hadn't included cut-and-paste layout, but that was all Kal could handle initially—to a Power Mac with the latest version of Quark and a printing press that wasn't half the size of the island.

Paul turned to the monitor on his own computer and stared at the headline. TOURISTS FOUND DEAD ON BEACH. He shuddered. When he first arrived on Malau years earlier, *he* had been a tourist, on vacation after graduating from Berkeley and before hitting the job market. He wound up staying and running the island's first "hometown" newspaper since being liberated from the Japanese and gaining independence after World War II.

What didn't make sense was how the two women died. The official cause of death was drowning, but they only drowned because they got tangled in a fishing net. According to the people they travelled with, one of them was an experienced scuba diver and swimmer. It didn't make sense that she and her friend had gotten so thoroughly tangled up in a net that, from all accounts, was just sitting there, moored into the sand.

The question now is, do we have the budget for a special followup edition? he thought. *No way do I wanna wait a week before doing the next one if something breaks.* Paul had wanted the paper to be daily in the first place, but the startup costs on a weekly were steep enough, and while he had the moral and legal support of the Malau government to produce a paper, he was on his own as far as funding went. He had only just paid off the initial loan, and—while pretty much the entire Malau population subscribed and ad revenues had increased steadily since he started—he barely broke even on a weekly, once you subtracted living expenses.

But then, how often do tourists die on the beach?

"Mail call!"

Paul started, then looked up to see Mak, Malau's lone postal employee, walking into Paul's office. "Oh, yipee," he said without enthusiasm. The vast majority of his posted mail consisted of junk or bills. On-island mail—in other words, the interesting stuff—generally came via fax or e-mail or was delivered in person.

"Actually," Mak said, dropping the rubber-banded bundle he held in his left hand into the wire in-box on Paul's desk, "there's one thing here you might like. From the States in a handwritten envelope."

Paul blinked. "Really? Where from?"

"I told you, the States."

"Geez, Mak, don't they teach you guys geography here?"

Mak looked mildly wounded. "Hey, I know all fifty states in the Union. What I don't know is what all those stupid two-letter codes mean. Dunno why they can't just write out the state names like sensible people. That entire country of yours is lazy."

Paul chuckled. "Yeah, yeah," he said as he grabbed the bundle, undid the rubber band and sifted through, looking for the mysterious envelope.

"Hey, you gonna write about those two girls that died?"

Nodding, Paul said, "Tonight's front page, actually."

"Yeah?"

Paul found what had to be the envelope, and was pleasantly surprised to see that it came from his college roommate, Kwame. "Yeah, well, it's news, y'know? And, by the way, for future reference, 'CA' is for California."

Mak smiled. "Right. Hey, when you gonna come over for dinner again? It's been over a month since the baby threw up on you. She misses it."

Laughing, Paul remembered playing with Mak's one-year-old girl and getting kid barf on his favorite T-shirt to show for it. But he also remembered Mak's amazing chili.

"Next week, okay?"

"Okay." Mak waved goodbye and went back to his appointed rounds.

Paul ripped open the letter from Kwame. *Dear Crazy Person*, it started, and Paul laughed. Kwame Davies had been a fellow Berkeley journalism student, and he and Paul had shared a room their final two years, graduating with visions of the *L.A. Times* dancing in their heads. Kwame had repeatedly told Paul that he was crazy to stay in "a third-world country" and that he was wasting his talents. However, he had limited those complaints of late to occasional jabs like letter greetings.

The missive itself brought Paul up to date on Kwame's life. Among other things, he had gotten a new apartment, a two-bedroom in Sherman Oaks, which he shared with a freelance photographer.

Paul set the letter down and looked out his office window at the clear blue sky, trees swaying in the gentle breeze. He thought about the three-bedroom house that he rented for a price that was less than half of Kwame's share of a no doubt cramped two-bedroom apartment. He thought about the fact that got to be his own editor, publisher, photographer, and reporter, responsible to no one but himself.

No regrets here, he decided, as he decided every day that he looked out over Malau.

He stored the file on his computer—*third-world countries don't have Power Macs*, he thought toward his friend thousands of miles away—and decided to go out for a walk on the beach, leaving the day's mail unread for once. The day of a new edition was always a slow one—he had dropped the disk containing the week's issue with Kal first thing in the morning; the paper would hit the stands by sunset—and Paul liked to spend it walking along the beach. Today was a particularly nice day for it.

He locked the office up and walked down to the nearest stretch of beach, removing his mocassins and holding them. Growing up in Los Angeles, he'd spent most of his life on beaches, but the nicest Malibu beach couldn't hold a candle to the crummiest one on Malau. Less crap in the sand, more blue in the water, less smog in the air.

Within fifteen minutes, he found himself not too far from where Marina Greenberg and Carol Franz met their deaths, and he shuddered.

Then his eye caught something interesting: an array of boxes and cases that looked more or less completely out of place on a beach. A little kid was rummaging through one of them, finally taking out something that looked like a tube. There was something that Paul was pretty sure was a tranquilizer gun strapped to the inside of the lid.

Either that kid is a thief, or he's got more aptitude than most ten-year-olds, Paul thought. *Whichever, this smells like news to me.*

The kid ran out toward the ocean, sloshing through the surf, and handed the tube thing to a tall man.

"Thanks," the man said without looking at the item, taking it with his left hand while holding some other kind of gadget in his right. The gadget took his attention for another couple of seconds before he finally looked at the tube the kid had given him. "Brandon, I said I wanted to measure water temperature—how do I do it with this?" The words were accompanied by a smile; a mild reprimand with no anger behind it. Paul noted that.

Brandon, for his part, didn't seem very reprimanded, so the light tone was just as well. He shrugged and said, "I goofed. Shoot me."

The man laughed, handing the tube back. "You're some assistant, pal."

"You get what you pay for, Dad."

A-ha, Paul thought, *a father-and-son team.* He walked toward the adult as Brandon dashed back to the boxes.

"I've been trying to figure out what you're doing, but I give up," he said.

The man didn't even turn to look at him. "Measuring water temperature."

"Interesting hobby," Paul said by way of a prompt.

Now the man turned to him. "I'm a marine biologist," he said with a smile.

"Oh, hey, sorry," Paul said, in case he had given offense with his hobby line. The wheels turned in his head. "Listen, how about giving me an interview?"

"You work for the local newspaper?"

Paul laughed. "I *am* the local newspaper." He extended his right hand. "Paul Bateman."

"Jack Ellway," the man said, returning the handshake. "This is my son, Brandon."

Paul turned around to see that Brandon had returned, this time holding something that, Paul assumed, would properly measure water temperature. Seeing that Brandon held the thing in his right hand, Paul switched his mocassins from his left hand and extended it for a handshake. "I'm Paul. How you doin'?"

As expected, Brandon had the weaker handshake one expected from the young—quick, light, and eager to be broken, not through any malice, but through wariness of strange adults. *Probably healthy*, Paul thought.

"Doin' okay," Brandon said, and handed the equipment to his father.

"Brandon's my intern," Jack said.

The kid seemed to wince, then gave Paul an almost conspiratorial look. "Intern means slave," he explained.

Paul couldn't help but laugh. He rembered his own internship in the summer between junior and senior years at Berkeley with a local magazine. Sometimes he felt that a slave would've been better off.

Brandon wandered away, and Paul turned to Jack. "What brings you to Malau?"

"The recent seismic activity. I want to study its effects on the area's marine life."

"This is great. I'm already doing a piece on a famous Australian geologist who's here to study—"

"Doctor Ralph Hale?" Jack interrupted.

Paul blinked. "You know him?" Hale was a minor celebrity in these parts—though the man himself would be the first to deny it—and Paul was almost done transcribing the interview with him that would run in one week.

"No, but I know his work."

"Well, maybe you'll get to meet him. In fact, I can probably introdu—"

"Hey, Dad, look at this!"

This last came from Brandon. Paul turned to see that

the kid had unearthed a large jacknife that was dark brown with rust. He started to open the knife up.

"Don't play with it, Brandon."

Even as Jack spoke, Brandon cut his finger on the blade. "Ow!"

Jack immediately ran over to his son, Paul behind him. As Jack grabbed Brandon's wrist to examine the finger more closely, Paul gingerly took the knife from the kid's other hand. He carefully closed the knife and put it in his shirt pocket.

"Are you gonna say 'I told you so'?" Brandon asked with the practiced here-we-go-again tone that kids often used with their parents. Paul himself had made a career out of using it with his own father.

"No, I'm gonna say 'tetanus shot.' "

"Can't you say 'I told you so' instead?"

Jack laughed. " 'Fraid not." He turned to Paul. "Where's the nearest emergency room?"

"Australia," Paul said without missing a beat. At Jack's aghast look, he quickly added, "No, I'm kidding. We've got a clinic on the island that's pretty complete. C'mon, I'll take you there."

He lead the pair to the edge of the beach, where Jack had a quick conversation with a young man regarding the boxes. The young man nodded—Paul was pretty sure he worked at the Ritz—and went off to take care of it.

The walk to the clinic was a short one down the island's main street. Brandon spent it holding his injured hand at the wrist and biting his lip. Jack asked, "Just a clinic? What happens for real emergencies?"

"Like I said, the place is pretty complete. For major surgery, or stuff like that, there's a big hospital on Kalor. Just a helicopter away. Don't worry, though, the clinic'll be fine. Actually, it's also run by an American—woman named Alyson Hart."

Jack looked like he was going to say something in

response to that, but they had arrived at the clinic. Like most of the buildings on Malau, it was a modest, one-story wooden structure, with the ground floor about half a foot above the earth as a caution against flooding. A Malauan nurse greeted Paul by name, asked Jack and Brandon some questions while putting a bandage on Brandon's finger, then told them to wait.

"What, no forms to fill out?" Jack asked as he took a seat on one of the couches.

Paul laughed. "They're not real big on forms 'round these parts. Back when I applied for permission to live here, the paperwork was minimal. The guy who put it through just shrugged and said, 'paperwork gives us gas.'"

Even Brandon smiled at that; prior to this, he'd been focusing on his finger.

The waiting room was empty when they arrived, but five more people came in right after them. The nurse dealt with each of them in turn. Within a few minutes, two women came out of the door adjacent to the waiting room, and then the nurse showed Paul, Jack, and Brandon into that same door.

It led to an examination room that had all the usual accoutrements: exam bed; scale; drawers full of various drugs, needles, medicines, and rubber gloves; various posters providing useful information on weight loss, the Heimlich maneuver, and anatomy on the wall; and a doctor, in this case a very attractive blonde in her early thirties.

As Alyson examined Brandon, Paul looked over at Jack and tried very hard to hide a grin. He recognized the look on Jack's face; it was the same one Paul had when he first met Dr. Alyson Hart. Paul had been completely smitten with her then. She was charming, bright, witty—and also completely uninterested in Paul Bateman, to his dismay. Not one to beat a dead horse, his pursuit of her stopped before it started, and he hoped they could at least be friends. Sadly, her lack of interest extended even to that; she was willing to talk to him professionally as a journalist, and respected what he was doing with the *Weekly News*, but refused to connect to him personally.

He wondered if Jack would have better luck.

After treating the wound itself, she prepared a needle for the tetanus shot. Brandon had spent the entire exam looking desultory and unhappy, though he answered all of Alyson's questions with clear answers and didn't act in the least bit surly. She dabbed a cotton ball in alcohol, rubbed it on his arm, and said, "Okay, this is gonna hurt a bit." Putting the cotton down, she picked up the needle and gave him the shot.

Brandon didn't even flinch. This time, Paul didn't bother to hide the grin.

"Didn't hurt?" Alyson sounded almost disappointed. "Must be losing my touch."

This, finally, got a rise out of the kid, and he smiled.

She continued, "Have your mom change the dressing tonight—"

"My mom's dead," Brandon said in a matter-of-fact tone that belied the information presented. He may as well have said she was back home in the States. Paul filed this bit of information away in the ever-growing compartment of his brain that he had labelled ELLWAY FAMILY.

"I'm sorry," Alyson said with inevitable awkwardness.

"Don't worry," Jack said lightly, "I know how to peel a Band-Aid."

Alyson looked almost relieved, which was obviously Jack's intention. *Good move*, Paul thought.

Jack continued, "How much do we owe you?"

Paul chuckled.

"Medical care's free on Malau," Alyson said.

Paul put in, "And worth every bit of it."

Alyson gave him a withering look. Paul just grinned. *So easy to get the good doctor's goat.*

"Okay," Jack said, "if we can't pay you, how about buying you lunch?"

Damn, Paul thought, *even I didn't move* that *fast*. He also noticed that Jack's posture had improved. On the beach and in the waiting room, he stood only moderately straight, but ever since he came into the exam room, he had practically dislocated his shoulders throwing them back.

To Paul's combined amusement and consternation, Alyson seemed to actually consider it, but then she looked out through the still-open door to the waiting room. Jack followed her gaze and nodded—and his shoulders returned to the slump of before.

"Some other time?" Alyson said.

The shoulders went back again. "Okay."

Alyson turned to Brandon. "And you be more careful with what you pick up on the beach, all right?"

Brandon nodded.

"Thanks, Doctor," Jack said, extending his hand.

"Please, it's Alyson," she said, returning the handshake. Father and son then went out to the waiting room. Paul noticed a moderate spring to Jack's step. *Better not tell him that Alyson tells everyone to call her by first name, whether she likes them or not. It'll just burst his bubble.*

" 'Bye, Alyson," he said with a jaunty wave to the doctor. Alyson simply nodded at him. Shaking his head, Paul followed the marine biologist and his assistant/intern/kid.

As they exited the air-conditioned clinic into a blast of hot and humid tropical air, Paul said, "I realize that I'm no Alyson Hart, but since she turned you down for lunch, mind breaking bread with me instead?"

"We probably should get back to work."

"Dad," Brandon said, managing to make it a three-syllable word. "The last meal we had was on the *plane*."

Paul grinned. Inviting Alyson to lunch obviously had

more to do with wanting to spend time with Alyson than actually eating anything. Just as obviously, that fact had gone completely over Brandon's prepubescent head, and he had gotten his hopes up for a real meal.

"As it happens," Paul said, "I can take you to the best restaurant on the island."

Jack glanced down at Brandon, who gave his father a pleading look, then grinned. "All right, then, let's eat."

"Great. Follow me."

They started down the main street toward Manny's. Paul had introduced many a new person to Malau in his time here, and he always made sure to at least direct them to Manny's Fine Food and Spirits, if not take them there himself. It was always worth it to see the looks on their faces when they found out who ran it. Besides, it really *was* the best food on the island.

"So," Jack said, "what's your story?"

Paul shrugged. "It's not much of a story. I graudated from Berkeley—degree in journalism—came here to do a little surfing before hitting the job market, and never left."

" 'Just came down for the weekend / But that was twenty-five years ago.' " Jack sang the words in a quiet voice.

Paul blinked. "Excuse me?"

Jack shook his head. "Sorry—just a lyric I heard in Key West a while back. How'd you end up running their newspaper?"

"They didn't *have* a paper when I got here. They thought, 'What's the point? Everybody already knows everybody's business.' But now they're real into it—everyone subscribes."

"They don't mind that you're American?"

Paul couldn't help but laugh at that. "See that over there?" He pointed at a flagpole in an intersection half a block away, on which flew not just the Malauan flag,

but the stars and stripes of the American flag right under
it. "They *love* Americans. We liberated them from the
Japanese."

"Really?"

Jack seemed genuinely surprised, both by the flag and
the information, which amazed Paul. *Geez, this stuff is all
over the brochures.* Then he remembered that Jack was
here to work, so he might've missed that.

"We still protect them," Paul said, using *we* to refer to
the United States despite his not having lived there for
years, "but from far enough away that they don't feel
Uncle Sam is breathing down their necks. There's not
even a military presence here—just one small unit stationed over on Kalor."

"That why Kalor rates a hospital?"

Paul laughed at that.

They arrived at Manny's shortly thereafter. A rhapsody
in rattan, the centerpiece was the gorgeous teakwood bar,
with rattan tables and chairs festooned around it. Nothing
about it said *fancy restaurant*, so newcomers were always
surprised, and initially dismayed, when Paul brought
them here. It looked for all the world like a glorified pub.

A very distinguished-looking man in his sixties
approached. "Hello, Paul," he said.

"Hiya, Manny. This is Jack Ellway and his son
Brandon."

"Welcome." He grabbed three menus and led the trio
to a table. "We have an excellent grilled grouper today,
and—"

A voice with a heavy New Zealand accent interrupted.
"Tell 'em who caught it, Manny."

Paul sighed as he took a seat opposite Jack. *Derek.
Great. Just great.* Had he known the brash expat would
be here, Paul would have suggested going to the Flying
Fish instead. But Paul had expected that Derek Lawson
would be out with his two cronies, Kikko and Naru, on

their little fishing trawler, showing tourists the finer points of netting lobster. *But then, after what happened yesterday, tourists are probably staying away from the water.* Instead, the three of them sat at the teakwood bar, sipping pints of beer.

"Derek caught it," Manny said unnecessarily while placing the menus on the table. "Our best catch is usually from Derek." Typically, Manny sounded completely neutral, neither praising Derek's skills nor condemning the fisherman's arrogance. Paul had always admired and envied that particular talent.

Derek hopped off his barstool and came over to the table, ignoring Paul completely—which suited the reporter just fine—and handed Jack a business card. "Welcome to Malau. If you're lookin' for the best deep-sea fishin' of your life, come out with Derek Lawson and crew." He gestured back at Kikko and Naru, who tipped their pints in acknowledgement.

Jack took the card and nodded politely. To Paul's glee, and Derek's apparent confusion, Jack seemed completely uninterested in what Derek had to offer. Paul, not a little smugly, said, "Mister Ellway is a marine biologist."

To his credit, Derek recovered well. "A man who knows his fish—even better." He tousled Brandon's hair, a gesture that, based on the kid's half-frown, half-snarl, he didn't appreciate in the least. "Kids're half-price."

He retreated to the bar and his crew. Manny then asked Jack, "You are staying on Kalor?"

"No, here on Malau. At the Ritz." As he spoke, a bus-boy placed three glasses of water on the table.

Manny nodded. "Our accomodations are modest by comparison…"

"This is where the tremors are. We prefer to be where the action is. I'm here to examine the effects of these tremors on the local marine life," he explained.

"Yes, well, we feel differently here. Our last 'action'

was World War II." He smiled a tiny smile, taking the edge off his statement. "When you are ready to order, Tari will take good care of you. I hope you enjoy your stay."

Paul noticed that Tari was taking someone else's order. "Thanks, Manny," he said.

Manny went off to a corner table, where various bits of paper were laid out.

"Nice old guy," Jack said as he reached for his water glass.

This was Paul's favorite part. "President Moki's a great father figure."

Jack did a spit-take with his water. Brandon started to laugh.

Paul grinned, and elaborated: "Manny's the President of Malau."

Dutifully wiping his chin with his napkin, Jack said dryly, "I'll leave a nice tip."

Before Paul could get into the rather interesting story of how a restaurant owner came to run the island, a tremor hit. The whole building started to shake. Most everyone tried to find something solid to hold onto, even if it was just a table. Paul himself didn't bother—a native Californian, he'd lived through much worse than this, and he could walk a straight line during a genuine quake, much less a comparatively wimpy tremor like this.

Naru, Paul noticed, wasn't so skilled; he fell off his stool. Kikko helped him back up just as the tremor died down.

"Cool," Brandon said.

Paul grinned. *Kids...*

TWO

Ralph Hale, Ph.D., bolted upright as the alarm on his watch sounded with an insistent *beep-beep* noise that would not cease until he pushed the tiny button on the watch's side. *Hell and damnation, but that thing's annoying*, he thought as he felt on his right wrist for the watch.

He couldn't find it.

Then, as awareness slowly penetrated his sleepy haze, he remembered that he had put the watch across the room precisely so he couldn't just switch it off and fall back asleep.

Gotta stop outsmarting myself, he thought with a chuckle as he clambered off the sofa where he had taken his nap. After a moment, he located the watch on the sideboard that served as his liquor cabinet and switched it off.

He gazed at the watch's digital display: 12:30. He still had half an hour before it was time to take the seismograph out from its underground—or under *sand*, really—hole. *Why would I set the alarm early and spoil a perfectly good nap, when—?*

Then his eye caught his battered old computer. *Right. Haven't checked the e-mail in almost two days.*

After switching the machine on—it took almost a full two minutes to boot up—he walked the short distance to the kitchen to turn on the burner under the kettle. He didn't really need the caffeine. Ralph Hale was a napper; he could go full-bore for four or five hours, crash for two, then be ready to go for another four hours. He had attained enough prominence as a geologist to be able to set his own peculiar hours, which is just how he liked it. Smiling as he dumped some herbal tea leaves into a strainer, he remembered his undergraduate days in Sydney, driving his roommates up the wall with his odd sleeping habits. *'Course, then there were the grad school days in Boston where everyone kept calling me "Oz," and that lovely tenure at Emory when everyone was browned off 'cause I didn't sound like Paul blasted Hogan.* Not that it was any better when he returned home to Australia. All the endless rules and regulations were enough to drive a man mad.

So finally he grew fed up and used the money he'd saved over the decades to put together the Hale Institute for Oceanography in Melbourne. He made his own damn rules and regulations.

One of those rules meant he could pick and choose his projects. The latest had him studying the unusual increase in seismic activity on and around Malau, his favorite of the numerous local islands. He could do what he was best at, do it how he wanted it done, and do it in a pleasant locale. As a result, he did excellent work, which made his Board of Directors at the Institute happy; and he got to take lots of naps, which made him happy. Hale's philosophy had always been that everyone should be as happy as possible, so this arrangement suited him just fine.

Eventually, the computer finished going through all eight million stages it needed to go through before it would allow its user to actually use it. *Times like this, I miss the old IBM PC. Couldn't do much more than a crummy word processor and a crummier database, but at least it booted up in thirty seconds.*

Hale double-clicked on the icon for his e-mail program, then single-clicked the CHECK MESSAGES icon. As the modem made the various and sundry awful noises it needed to make to connect Hale's computer to the Internet (or, at least, to his e-mail provider's little corner of it), he noticed another icon for the program he checked Usenet with. *Better not get into that*, he decided. *The e-mail alone'll take the whole time.* Sometimes he wondered why he bothered with the various newsgroups that discussed geology (his chosen field) and scuba diving (his favorite hobby), since ninety-eight percent of what was posted there was either useless and/or inaccurate. *Still, that other two percent can be gold.*

He winced as the program informed him that he had three hundred and sixty-two messages. The program also sorted it for him. The stuff from the various mailing lists could wait until later; that accounted for eighty percent of the messages right there. Of the balance, he recognized only a few e-mail addresses, and only three absolutely required a response. One was from the dive shop, informing him that his new air tanks had arrived and when did he want to pick them up? Another was from Paul Bateman, saying he'd have the transcription of the interview for Hale to go over in a couple of days.

The third was from his editor at *Scientific American*, who was justifiably annoyed at his tardiness in delivering his latest column. *Hell and damnation*, he thought with a sigh. The seismic activity in the local waters had gone into overdrive, and he'd spent every waking moment—and, if it came to that, every napping moment—trying to figure out why. His quarterly column for *SA* had gone straight out of his mind.

A whistling sound from the kitchen grabbed his attention. He wandered back into the kitchen, switched the burner off, and poured the water into the waiting mug. He contemplated several options, most of which boiled down to coming up with some kind of excuse. He even briefly entertained the notion of using those two poor sheilas drowning the previous night, then immediately rejected the idea as tasteless and irresponsible.

Walking back to the computer and setting the steeping tea on a coaster next to it, he decided to just go for the truth. Sighing, he hit the REPLY button and typed, *Sorry, love, been a bit crazy hereabouts. By Friday, I promise. Cheers, Ralph.*

None of the e-mails were the one he truly wanted to see: the one from his old friend Andrew Angelopoulos, a marine biologist from Queensland. He'd gone on walkabout at the beginning of the semester, but Hale remembered him as an obsessive net-head. He thought for sure that Angelopoulos would check his e-mail, but he hadn't replied to any of the messages Hale had sent over the past week. *Pity. Could use a marine biologist's input right about now.*

He took one last quick glance over the various mailing list messages to see if any subject lines looked familiar—sure enough, a few did, and he read those, and started composing replies to one or two. One in particular was a pronouncement made by some know-nothing undergraduate about sharks that Hale couldn't just let go by without a severe reprimand from someone who actually knew what he was talking about.

After a minute, he glanced at his watch—which read 1:02. His tea had gone cold and he was late.

Hell and damnation, this contraption'll be the death of me. He quit out of the e-mail program, shut the computer down, gulped down the last of his tea, grabbed a small shovel, and headed out to the beach.

Outside, it was another hot and humid day, as would be expected for a South Seas island. Hale loved it. Well, not the humidity, but other things made up for it—unlike, say, Atlanta, where he had spent many years as a geology professor, and where the humidity seemed all-encompassing.

He walked the short distance from the bungalow the Institute had rented to the beach where he'd buried the prototype seismograph. On the way, he saw a much lower concentration of people than one would expect on such a beautiful day. Hale thought again about the two American girls who drowned. *Poor sheilas, going on vacation and winding up like that.*

Not everyone had been intimidated by the news of drowning tourists—Hale saw a man, woman, and a little bloke who couldn't have been more than eight eating a picnic lunch, and another man playing Frisbee with his dog. *'Course, maybe they didn't hear about what happened*, Hale thought, then dismissed it. It was possible, of course, but not likely. News travelled faster than the wind on Malau.

Another little bloke was watching the picnicking family with a peculiar interest. Hale noticed that the boy was holding, of all things, a water thermometer—and also that he had a longing expression on his face. Hale wondered what had brought that on.

Stop trying to figure out other people's lives, he admonished himself, shaking his head, *and get on with the work.*

Ralph Hale had a phenomenal memory, and so moved unerringly to the very spot where he had buried the seismograph twenty-four hours earlier. Kneeling down into the sand, he started digging with the shovel until he found the latest toy from his techies at the Institute. Once the shovel struck the metal of the seismograph's container, he set it aside and pushed the remaining sand away with his hands.

Inevitably, his action caught someone's eye—a young man approached just as Hale finished unearthing the device.

"Is that some kind of seismograph?" the man asked.

Hale looked up sharply at the man. He had spoken with an American accent, and Hale saw that he held a couple of sample jars. "Yeah," he said. "Excellent guess. It's just a prototype, mind you."

"Great toy. Doctor Hale, I presume?"

Hale stood up. "Another good guess," he said. This time he wasn't surprised; anyone bright enough to recognize the seismograph for what it was would probably know Hale was on the island.

"I've read your articles, and your column in *Scientific American*. I'm a marine biologist—Jack Ellway."

"Ralph Hale," he replied automatically, then shook the man's hand. "You know that, of course. Never mind." *A marine biologist*, he thought, remembering several unanswered e-mails from Angelopoulos. *Well, the hell with you, old friend, I've got someone close to home now.* "I'm glad you're here, actually—I've been wanting to get a perspective from someone on your end of things about all this seismic activity."

"Well, the water temperature's changing, for one thing, which could affect migratory patterns. I've got my son checking some of that now."

Hale remembered the little bloke with the water thermometer. "That's your son?"

Ellway smiled. "Yeah, and my intern—well, he prefers 'assistant.' Either way, he's very bright. A lot better than most of the other losers I've had as interns, believe me."

"Yeah, well, I had enough of that when I was teaching undergraduates. That's why I usually work alone now. Besides, I like to get my own hands dirty." Realizing they were getting off track, Hale steered the conversation back to migratory patterns. "Have you noticed any particular shifts?"

"I only just arrived today, so I haven't had time to do any kind of serious projections, but I think we can expect certain…"

Brandon looked wistfully as a woman wiped her son's face with a napkin. At least, Brandon figured they were a family. They certainly looked like a family.

They look like us.

He remembered the Key West trip. On their last day there, after Mom and Dad had completed their work (days ahead of schedule, as it happened), they had thrown together a picnic on the beach. Brandon hadn't much liked the Key West beach—not wide enough, and the waves were all wimpy—but they had had a great time. They hadn't had sandwiches, though—Mom had put together a bunch of different fish plates.

Aside from that, though, these three people were dead ringers for the Ellway family in Key West.

We'll never have that kind of picnic again.

Then: *Stop it! They're probably not even a real family. Probably just some lady and her nephew and some guy she met at a bar somewhere or something like that. You don't know that they're a real family.*

Having convinced himself of that, Brandon went on toward the rocks where Dad had asked him to take the water temperature. He looked back to see Dad talking to some older guy. Whatever they were talking about, Dad was really into it. *The old dude's gotta be a scientist.* Dad didn't get that look on his face unless he was talking about work. Certainly, he never looked like that during lunch with Paul, though Paul was certainly nice enough.

Out of the corner of his eye, Brandon noticed a guy throwing a Frisbee toward the water, a dog going after it. The guy who threw it winced as the Frisbee glided over into the surf. *Probably overthrew it*, Brandon thought. *Mom always got that look on her face when she overthrew a Frisbee back when we used to—*

Stop thinking about it!

The guy ran toward the water even as the dog obediently ran into the crashing waves to retrieve the Frisbee—suddenly, the dog turned around and ran out of the water, making little *yipe yipe* noises.

The guy met his dog halfway, and knelt down to ruffle its now wet fur. "What's the matter, boy?"

Of course, the dog didn't answer, so the guy looked out to the ocean to see if he could see what the dog saw.

Curious, Brandon followed the guy's gaze.

Suddenly, something poked its head out of the water, just for a second. All Brandon could really see were a what looked like a horn and a pair of eyes. It might've been a carnival mask, like the ones he'd seen in New Orleans.

But carnival masks didn't usually have scales.

They didn't usually blink, either.

The guy looked at Brandon, his eyes wide. "Did you see that?"

"Yeah. What was it?"

"I dunno." He turned back to the ocean.

Brandon did the same, but the thing had disappeared, and nothing else poked out from the water.

"Weird. Maybe it was nothing," Brandon said.

"Maybe," the guy said. "Sure spooked Fred here." He looked down at the dog, which still looked frightened out of its mind. "Hey, c'mon boy, it's okay," the guy said, scratching the dog behind the ears.

Brandon, meanwhile, went on to the rocks. *Maybe I did imagine it.*

Yeah, right. So did that guy and his dog. Still, it was probably just some kind of fish or amphibian or something. Brandon was pretty good at recognizing marine life at this point, but he had hardly gotten a good enough look at whatever it was to identify it.

He went to perform the task his father had set him and put the creature out of his mind.

"You're going out windsurfing? *Tonight?* What're you, nuts?"

Kulani sighed. She had been hoping that her father would work late tonight so that she and Dak could go out without a lecture, but no such luck.

"I'm not nuts, Pop. Dak and I planned this two days ago, and we're going."

"What about those two girls—"

"Pop, just because two beach bimbos were too stupid to stay out of a fishing net doesn't mean Dak and I shouldn't go out."

Pop glared at Kulani. She was worried that he'd try to forbid her from going. It wouldn't work, of course—Kulani was an adult, and he had no right to control her movements. She was only living with him until she and Dak got married anyhow.

Finally he said, "They weren't beach bimbos, they were from Minnesota. And one of them was an experienced diver. It was in the paper."

Kulani rolled her eyes. "Pop, they're just a couple of dumb tourists. I'm a grown woman who's been windsurfing since I was two, and it's a beautiful night out."

Pop walked up to her and put his hands on her shoulders. In a much softer voice, he said, "Lani, I just want you to be safe."

Her anger melted and she sighed, kissing Pop on the forehead as she said, "Don't worry, Pop, I'll be careful." Then she hugged him.

A knock came from the front door. "Hello?" It was Dak.

"Dak!" Kulani broke her father's embrace and ran to

the man she loved. She almost leapt into his arms; she did kiss him. She hadn't seen him in almost a full day, and she had been counting the moments until she saw him again.

She couldn't wait to be married to him so that she would see him all the time.

"Ready to go?" he said after she finally paused for breath.

"Definitely."

Pop said, "You two be careful out there, okay?"

In a deferential voice, Dak said, "Don't worry, sir, we will." Dak had always been good about being on his best behavior around Pop. It was one of several reasons why Pop blessed their engagement.

"C'mon, let's go," Kulani said, pulling on Dak's arm, trying to drag him out the door. His battered blue pickup truck was parked out front, the two sets of surf skis in the cab. "What took you so long?" she asked as she got into the passenger's side seat. "I thought I'd have to listen to Pop bitching and moaning about the dangers of the water for *hours*."

Dak laughed as he got in on his side. "Since when does your father think it's dangerous to go in the water?"

"Since two dumb Americans couldn't figure out how to get out of a fishing net."

"Well, he's not the only one spooked," Dak said as he started the truck. It stalled. "Derek didn't get a single ride today—spent the whole day in Manny's."

"Manny must've *loved* that."

Dak tried to start the truck again. This time, it stayed on, and they drove off to the beach. "Anyhow, practice ran a little late. Maru was being little Mister Perfectionist again."

Kulani smiled. Dak was in Friends Anemones, the house band at Rik's Bar and Grill; he played bongos and other percussion, and was quite good at it. They were hoping to get some gigs on some of the other islands, maybe even in Sydney or Melbourne or Manila.

The trip to the beach took only a few minutes—they wouldn't have bothered with the vehicle at all if it weren't for the skis. Dak simply left the car at a spot a short walk from the shore—parking regulations were rather loose on Malau—and they got out.

Kulani moved to the back of the truck, as did Dak. She waited for Dak to open the cab door, but instead he took her in his arms and kissed her.

The kiss took some time—how long, Kulani did not know, nor did she much care. All she cared about was Dak.

"Have I told you recently how beautiful you are?" Dak asked after the kiss ended.

"It's been *hours*."

"Much too long, then," he said, and kissed her again. After this last kiss, he smiled, opened the truck, and grabbed a pair of skis.

A small frown on her face, Kulani did likewise with the other pair.

When they reached the edge of the surf, they set the skis down. Before Dak could do anything else, Kulani leaned over and kissed him. Dak was only surprised for a moment, then he returned the kiss.

After they broke it, Kulani waited expectantly—but Dak pushed off into the water. Sighing, Kulani followed.

Within a few minutes, they were in the middle of the ocean, the salt spraying on their faces, the stars shining in the sky, and Kulani staring at Dak's lovely back.

That back then pivoted and turned, and Kulani looked up to see Dak staring at her. "You're so beautiful."

Finally, she thought, smiling. She imagined that she glowed in the moonlight.

Suddenly, Dak lost his balance—unusual, in and of

itself, since Dak had almost perfect balance. Then she started to glide past him.

For some reason, Dak was dead in the water.

"Dak?"

Rather than answer, Dak looked down at his skis. Kulani followed his gaze to the rope attached to the back of the skis, which was, peculiarly, taut.

Kulani looked back up at Dak, but he looked as confused as she. She was about to ask him what was going on, when suddenly, she found herself moving farther away from him, faster. *But that doesn't make sense.*

Then she realized that she wasn't moving faster—Dak was being pulled *backwards*.

"Oh, my God," Dak said.

Kulani was frozen with indecision—not to mention necessity. Unlike Dak, she had a much harder time keeping her balance, and if she tried to turn around, or maneuver in some other way, she would probably fall into the ocean. *Oh, God, what do I do?*

Dak's skis were moving faster now, and farther away from her. "Help me!" he cried.

A fist of ice closed over Kulani's heart as Dak finally did lose his balance and fell into the water.

"Dak!"

As he fell, his head hit one of the skis with a sickening *thud*.

"Dak!"

With that cry, Kulani lost her balance and fell into the water. She thrashed about for a minute before getting her bearings and breaking through to the surface. She swam over to one of Dak's skis and found purchase on it.

"Dak! Dak!"

Then she saw the blood.

"Nooooooo!"

More blood, so much that the water turned the color of

red wine. So much that Kulani thought she'd drown in it.

She screamed.

She screamed until her throat went raw.

Finally, she stopped screaming and started to cry.

Then Dak's body floated up to the surface, and the screaming started again.

THREE

Until arriving on Malau, Jack Ellway had never met a head of state. Since arriving, he'd not only met one, but eaten at his restaurant, and now was having dinner with him. He found he was rather enjoying the experience. The fact that said head of state had asked to join him, his son, and Ralph Hale in a humble manner uncharacteristic of most politicians helped, as did the fact that the president's chosen topic of conversation was Jack's work.

Toward the end of the meal, Manny said, "Fascinating. If it is not too impertinent, who is paying for all of this?"

Jack swallowed a bite of his delicious boiled mud crab before answering. "Well, I'm working on a partial grant from UCSD. Sorry, that's the University of—"

"California at San Diego, yes, I know. I received a Master's in English Literature from their Revelle College," Manny said.

"Uh, right." That, like so many things about the Malauan president, surprised Jack. The image he had formed of Manny Moki kept being thrown for a loop with each new revelation.

"So you live in La Jolla?" Manny asked, referring to the San Diego suburb where UCSD's campus was located.

"No, we're in San Diego proper, though we haven't gotten back there much the last few months."

"Interesting. I must thank you, Mr. Ellway, for indulging an old man's tedious questions."

"Oh, not at all," Jack said, taking a final bite of his mud crab.

"Dad *loves* talking about work," Brandon said with a roll of his eyes.

Hale laughed. "Occupational hazard, I'm afraid."

Manny looked down at Jack's now-empty plate. "I see you enjoyed the mud crabs."

"*Enjoyed* is too mild a word. I've never had anything like this. They're *delicious*."

Brandon asked, "Did Derek catch these, too?"

Manny smiled politely. "It isn't necessary to send out large fishing boats to catch mud crabs—you may grab them freely from the surf. In fact—"

The president cut himself off at the sound of sirens.

At first, Jack thought very little of the noise. Born in New York City and raised there and in Chicago before settling in San Diego after college, sirens had always been part of the background noise for him growing up, so he barely registered their presence anymore.

Manny, however, seemed to think it was a big deal, as did Hale, who put down his fried tuna and stood up.

A couple of people went outside, then someone ran back in and said breathlessly, "It's Kulani with the chief—and there's a body in the back—I think it's Dak!"

That started a commotion.

"What?"

"It can't be!"

"I just *saw* Dak at practice."

"Did she kill him?"

"Oh, my God."

A tide of humanity swept toward the door, and Jack, Brandon, Hale, and Manny went with it.

The siren belonged to a jeep, of all things, with the word POLICE stencilled on the side. *Given how little of this island is paved, that's probably the most practical vehicle to use for emergencies*, Jack mused. A man in his thirties drove the jeep—presumably Police Chief Joe Movita—and a woman sat on the passenger side, wrapped in a blanket. They came to a halt in front of the clinic.

"Dak and Kulani are a couple of kids," Doctor Hale explained as they walked briskly toward the clinic, along with a few dozen others, both from Manny's and elsewhere. "Dak's in one of the local bands. He and Kulani were gonna be married in a few weeks."

"Damn," Jack muttered.

As they approached, Jack heard a trembling voice. It was the woman in the passenger seat—Kulani—sounding like she was in a daze.

"Something…pulled him backwards…something in the water…some *thing*…"

Jack and Doctor Hale held back, Jack holding Brandon's hand. They were outsiders here, after all, and he could see fine over the heads of the others. He and Hale would just get in the way of the professionals if they tried to get involved any more.

Speaking of whom, Alyson ran out of the clinic, two orderlies on her heels. The police chief indicated the body in the back. The doctor pulled the sheet back.

Jack held down a gag reflex as she did so. The body looked like it had been *chewed*.

"What do you think, Jack?" Hale asked. "Dolphin? Whale?"

Hale spoke in a detached, professional manner, for which Jack was grateful—it gave him a chance to get his bearings. "Either one would be way off course for this time of year."

"Which would be consistent with your theories about the impact of the seismic activity, yeah?"

Before Jack could answer, he noticed Brandon trying to stand on tiptoe to get a better look. "I can't see. What's going on?"

Unbidden, images of that horrible day over a year earlier flowed into Jack's mind: Doctor Bottroff telling Diane Ellway why she was having those awful headaches; Diane telling Jack in that stoic manner with which she always imparted bad news; trying to make their eleven-year-old son understand, using words like *inoperable* and *brain tumor*, that Mom wasn't going to be around much longer, never quite able to use the word *dying*; watching as Diane deteriorated, her hair falling out from the chemotherapy; trying to wake her up that one morning and realizing she wasn't breathing....

Jack shook his head to clear the images. *The last thing Brandon needs is to be exposed to more death.* He put his hand on his son's shoulder and said, "I think you'd better go back to the hotel, Brandon."

"Nah, I'm okay," Brandon said with the self-assuredness of the twelve-year-old who's already seen everything.

In fact, he's already seen this, after a fashion, which is exactly why I want him out of here. "I wasn't really giving you a vote," he said gently, giving Brandon's shoulder a squeeze. "Go on, I'll be there soon."

Brandon looked extremely unhappy, but said nothing and obediently headed back toward the Ritz.

Once Brandon was out of sight, Jack started to move in closer to the crowd surrounding Dak's body, Hale close behind. Alyson had done a quick examination of the body and replaced the blanket. As the two orderlies carried the bodies inside, Alyson put her arm around Kulani, who still seemed to be in a daze.

"Kulani?" Alyson said gently.

At this, Kulani looked up and fixed Alyson with an expression that made Jack's heart crumple. He knew that face. *It's the same face that looked back at me in the mirror for months after Diane died.*

Alyson led Kulani inside. He hoped that she would show Kulani the same compassion that she showed to a twelve-year-old with a cut finger.

"D'you know what happened?" Hale said. Jack was about to ask the geologist how Jack could possibly know when he'd spent most of the last five hours with Hale himself, when he realized that the question had been asked of Paul Bateman, who was walking over from the police jeep.

Paul's presence was hardly a surprise. The third death in two nights certainly qualified as news. "Joe told me that something grabbed Dak's surf skis and pulled him backward. Dragged him through the water. He also told me earlier that, according to their investigation, something dragged the fishing net that those two women drowned in last night. Might be related."

"I don't know," Jack said, "but I think there's something unusual out there. Some kind of marine life that doesn't belong here." He remembered Brandon's story, told at the beginning of dinner, of a weird head that poked briefly out of the water that afternoon. "Certainly, whatever attacked Dak isn't native to these parts at this time of year."

Hale rubbed his chin thoughtfully. "We could go up in my plane tomorrow, scan the waters, see what we see."

Jack almost sighed. *Wish I had the kind of funding that let me talk casually about "my plane,"* he thought with a silent curse at UCSD's bean counters. Aloud, he simply said, "Great." He walked over to where the president was standing, talking with the police chief. "President Moki," he said—the old man had politely asked Jack to call him

"Manny," since, as he said, "everyone else does," but Jack couldn't bring himself to do so, particularly now—"it might be wise to keep everyone out of the water until we know what we're dealing with."

"This is nonsense," came a voice from behind Jack. He saw Derek Lawson approaching.

"Perhaps it would be wise," Manny said, ignoring Derek. "At least, until we find out what killed our friend Dak."

"They were surfing at *night*," Derek said with a bark of unkind laughter. "Stupidity killed him."

Taking the president's lead, Jack ignored Derek, and asked, "You'll keep the waters clear?"

"How long will it take you to survey them?"

Kikko, who, along with Naru, flanked Derek, muttered, "If we can't fish, we can't get paid."

"C'mon, Manny," Derek said, "don't let outsiders push you around. This is *our* island."

For the first time, the president looked at the fisherman. "Excuse me, Derek, but I believe that New Zealand is *your* island." He spoke in the same even, polite tone that he used at all times, but Jack could tell that he would also brook no further commentary on the subject.

Before the argument could continue, a hush fell over the area. Red Sea–like, the crowd parted for a man as old as President Moki, dressed in the collar of a Christian minister or priest.

Nodding to the old man, Moki said, "Father Rauh."

The priest simply nodded in return, then entered the clinic.

Moki turned to the chief of police, whose jaw was set so tightly Jack almost thought he'd broken it recently. "What do you think?" the president asked him.

"About closing the waters?" The chief rubbed his not-really-broken jaw. "Normally, I'd say no, but we've got three suspicious deaths which might be related—"

"Might?" Paul interrupted. "C'mon, Joe, it's kinda obvious that they—"

The chief interrupted right back, "Yes, Paul, *might*. The two causes of death are different, and kindly don't pull that all-knowing-reporter-makes-fun-of-dumb-cop crap on me, all right?"

Paul seemed taken aback. "Sorry."

Joe turned back to the president. "But I've also been getting reports all day about weird sightings in the ocean. Much higher than the usual, and they're all pretty similar."

"A large reptilian head with a small horn at the center," Jack said.

Everyone—except for Hale and the president—turned to him. "Yes," Joe said, only momentarily surprised. "You saw it, too?"

"No, but my son did."

Derek finally spoke up again: "So, based on two dumb tourists, one dumb local, and a boogey man, you're gonna shut us down?" *Knew the silence was too good to last*, Jack thought.

Before anyone could answer, Alyson came out of the clinic. She removed a pair of latex gloves with a telltale *snap* and placed them in the pockets of her lab coat.

"What did you find, Doctor?" the president asked.

Alyson took a breath before answering. "Well, keeping in mind that I don't have the facilies, nor the qualifications, to do a proper autopsy…" Manny nodded in understanding and she went on: "Based on initial observation, I'd say he died of severe blood loss, possibly also trauma to major organs. He also had a blunt trauma to the head, but I don't think that contributed."

"Jibes with what Kulani said," the chief put in. "She said he hit his head on the skis as he fell in."

"We'll need to ship the body to Kalor for a proper autopsy. However, I can tell you for sure that the blood loss was due to several bites all over his body."

Hale asked, "What kind of bites?"

"That's the weird part," Alyson said, blowing out a breath. "I have seen bites from every type of animal known to this island and its surrounding waters, and I have never seen *anything* that matches this."

Jack turned to the president, an expectant look on his face. To his mind, Alyson's report simply confirmed that the waters should be closed until he could investigate.

If the gravity of the decision weighed heavily on President Moki, he didn't show it. Jack had the crazy thought that he'd never want to play poker with the man. He simply looked thoughtful for a moment, then said, "Very well. For the time being, no sea craft are to sail from Malau's shores." He turned to Joe. "See to it."

The chief nodded and moved off to his jeep.

Derek threw up his hands. "I don't bleedin' *believe* this! Manny, this is nuts, we—"

"I have made my decision, Derek," the president said, his calm inversely proportional to the fisherman's anger.

Hale stepped between Jack and the two other men, as if to say, *Let these two hash out their own problems—we've got our own.* "We'll have to leave at first light."

Jack nodded. "Brandon and I'll meet you at the airport at dawn." *Airport*, he thought, *right. It's a one-story building and a strip of tarmac.*

Hale made an odd face, like he had news he didn't want to impart. "Actually, what I've got is a seaplane; it's out at the pier. And I'm afraid it's only a two-seater. No room for the little bloke."

Disappointed, Jack nodded again. *Brandon would've enjoyed coming along,* he thought. *Ah, well. He's a bright kid. He'll understand.*

"I don't understand," Brandon said the next morning in the hotel room.

He had been asleep by the time Jack finally got back. He and Hale had talked to the police chief some more about the various sightings, all of which were indeed eerily similar to Brandon's quick glance the day before. Then they'd gone to Hale's bungalow to hastily map out an itinerary for their flyby.

Jack outlined the game plan while he tossed a few items into a backpack. Brandon was thrilled right up until the part when Jack told the boy he couldn't come along.

"This isn't fair," Brandon continued. "I always get to go along with you on stuff."

"I know—I'm sorry," he said, meaning it. "But Doctor Hale's plane is just a two-seater."

"How come when you need me I'm your 'assistant,' but when you don't need me, I'm just your kid?"

Jack shook his head. Brandon was so mature, so capable, that sometimes Jack forgot that he was still a twelve-year-old boy. *I should've known better than to expect a grown-up reaction. He's a kid—how would a kid react to this?*

He thought back to himself as a twelve-year-old, and how he felt on vacations with his family. Usually, the parts he looked forward to was when they'd go off to do something he thought was boring and they'd leave him alone to fend for himself. *So let's try that approach.*

"You've got a whole day to run around the island on your own. No responsibilities." *No money, either*, he remembered, then fished in his pocket for cash, pulling out a ten-dollar bill. Luckily, American currency was good on Malau—indeed, Paul had said the day before that the local merchants preferred American dollars to Malauan ones. "You can buy yourself lunch at Manny's, and then you can take the camcorder and go exploring—"

"I thought I was 'on my own,' " Brandon said, defiantly. "Why're you telling me what to do?"

Jack realized that he wasn't going to win no matter

what, so he held up his hands in surrender—the ten bucks still in his right hand. "Fine, whatever. I was just making a suggestion." He handed Brandon the ten.

Brandon just looked at it, then back up at his father. "This is supposed to last me all day?" He had a smirk on his face.

Intimately familiar with that smirk, and taking it as a conciliatory sign, Jack returned it with a grin, and fished out another ten.

As Brandon took the two bills, Jack's grin fell, and he put on his most serious expression. "And stay out of the water."

"Okay," Brandon said casually.

"I mean it, Brandon." He put his hands on his son's shoulders. "Leaving aside the danger from whatever might be out there, it's illegal to go into the water right now. I'd hate for Paul's next front page to be AMERICAN SCIENTIST'S INTERN—"

"Assistant," Brandon corrected.

Jack smiled. "Fine—AMERICAN SCIENTIST'S ASSISTANT JAILED ON CHARGES OF STUPIDITY."

Brandon laughed. "Okay, Dad, I'll be careful, don't worry."

"Good." He kissed Brandon on the head and let go of his shoulders. "President Moki gave us until sunset, so I'll be back by then."

Brandon wandered aimlessly down the main beach of Malau. For most of the morning, he sat in the hotel room, sulking and reading through a couple of his prized *Captain Marvel*s. Around noon, though, his stomach started to rumble, so he followed Dad's advice and had lunch at Manny's, which turned out to be a mistake. Derek and the Derek-ettes were once again seated at the bar swilling beer and being obnoxious. They didn't actually bother Brandon—and, thank God, Derek didn't come over and toussle Brandon's hair again—but they looked at him like everything was his fault. Derek did talk to some of the other people sitting around, who looked pretty upset. *Probably other people who wanted to be in the water*, Brandon figured. Manny wasn't there either, so the atmosphere was real unpleasant.

Thanks for leaving me behind, Dad, he thought, annoyed.

He ate lunch quickly, then took the camcorder he had retrieved from one of the duffels and decided to wander around the beach. He started from where he and Dad had been doing their initial work, picked a direction, and walked. Occasionally, he filmed something that looked interesting: a peacock spreading its tail here, a flock of birds there. At one point, he saw a few dolphins frolicking, jumping into the air in tiny arcs. He videotaped that, remembering that Mom always loved dolphins.

Stop thinking about that.

After about ten minutes, the sand started getting rockier. He looked ahead to see that foliage started to creep into the beach as the coastline veered sharply to the left. Brandon recalled from their flight in that one end of Malau was jungle—it covered a little less than quarter of the island. It wasn't much of a jungle, as jungles went; but, as Dad had said in the plane, it added to the island's character.

Sighing, he shifted the camcorder to his left hand, picked up a few pebbles with his right, and started skimming them into the water.

His uncle had shown him how to skim pebbles like this when Brandon was six and they visited him in Pennsylvania. "Gotta throw sidearm," Uncle Scott used to say, "just like Kent Tekulve." To this day, Brandon had no idea who Kent Tekulve was, but he kept practicing throwing sidearm until he could make almost any pebble skip at least four times before sinking.

It was after he made one nice flat pebble go seven times that he saw it.

At first he thought, crazy as it was, that one of his pebbles had turned around and was coming back.

Then it came out of the water and zipped into the foliage.

Brandon couldn't really make out what it was, but it was green, and it was big. In fact, he was pretty sure that it was the same color green as that thing he saw the previous day in the water.

It's probably just a salamander or something, he thought, but salamanders didn't usually come that large.

He considered his options. Following the blur meant going into the jungle. He had no idea what lay within it. On the other hand, how dangerous could it be? And Dad didn't tell him not to go into the jungle, just not to go into the water.

And he did say I should go exploring.

Of course, Dad had suggested eating at Manny's in the same breath, and that had turned out really lousy, but Brandon didn't care. He wanted to see what that thing was.

These thought processes took all of a second, so he muttered, "Shazam," and dashed into the foliage on the heels of the green blur.

Though he did not possess the speed of Mercury that his hero had, Brandon could move quickly even through the dense, big-leafed trees around him. The plants ahead of him rustled, and he followed the sounds as they led him deeper and deeper.

Just as the rustling stopped, Brandon came to an overhanging tree whose branches drooped down like the flaps of a tent. He pushed the leaves aside to find himself at the mouth of a beautiful lagoon.

Like all the water hereabouts, the lagoon was a deep blue.

However, it wasn't an undisturbed blue—right at the shoreline near Brandon's feet, the water rippled, as if something had just dashed into the water.

Brandon smiled. *The wisdom of Solomon tells me that the little dude ran in here.* He squatted down and peered into the water.

Suddenly, a creature emerged from the water. To Brandon's amazement, it actually did look like a salamander, with two major differences. For one thing, salamanders didn't walk on their hind legs; for another, they rarely grew three feet long.

Its eyes were huge, like some goofy stuffed animal's.

Then it went back into the water.

"Holy moley," Brandon muttered.

He stared at the water for several minutes, wondering when the thing would come back out.

The ripples it made started to slow down. After a little while, the water was completely calm.

Of the creature, there was no sign.

Weird, Brandon thought.

Jack Ellway's first thought upon seeing Ralph Hale's seaplane was, *I've got to get my own oceanographic institute. UCSD would never let me have toys like this.* He directed a few more choice thoughts toward his employers as the dinghy took them to where Hale kept his plane.

They spent the day flying around the open ocean, Jack peering through a pair of binoculars, trying to find something that didn't match with the information regarding local marine life that he'd studied in depth in preparation for his trip here. Hale, for his part, steered the plane unerringly; Jack only felt queasy three or four times, which was a lot less than he expected in so small a plane with such high winds.

Around lunchtime, they landed on Kalor to grab a quick lunch—Jack was not surprised to find that every-

one they met knew Hale personally—then went out
again.

By late afternoon, they had given up. "I haven't seen a
damn thing that doesn't belong here," he shouted to Hale
in the front compartment.

"Pity," he said. "I'll radio the pier, let 'em know we're
comin' in."

It took another ten minutes for them to arrive back at
Malau, and another five to take the dinghy back to the
pier.

Shortly after meeting him, Hale had commented to
Jack that, "You can't order a pint on one end of Malau
without someone on the other end knowin' what brand
you're drinkin' inside of two seconds." So it came as no
surprise to find a massive welcoming committee waiting
for them at the pier: President Moki, Paul Bateman, Chief
Movita, and a number of others, including, inevitably,
Derek Lawson and his two hangers-on.

Before the dinghy pilot could even tie the boat down,
Paul asked, "Did you see anything?"

Jack shook his head and he climbed out of the dinghy
onto the wooden pier. "Nothing unusual—at least, nothing near the surface."

Hale jumped out behind Jack. Sounding completely
undaunted, in direct contrast to Jack, he said, "Sonar
would give us a better idea. My institute has a ship that's
equipped with—"

"Oh, for God's sake." That, of course, was Derek, who
looked at the president. "You see, Manny, it's all nonsense. Lift the ban right now, this minute."

What a selfish bastard, Jack thought. Three people had
been killed, and all this idiot could think about were his
lousy fishing revenues. Forcing himself to remain calm,
he said, "I think it should remain. Just another couple of
days, till—"

Derek whirled around to face Jack, looking furious.

"*You* think? *You* think! Who the hell are *you*, ordering everyone about?"

Stay calm, Jack, don't let him get to you. Speaking very slowly, he replied, "I'm just trying to help."

Derek made a dismissive noise and said, "Yeah, help yourself. Big-shot scientist struttin' around here like you own the place. You and your smartass kid, goin'—"

That did it. Jack grabbed Derek by his T-shirt and said, "Watch your mouth, pal!"

Derek shoved Jack, forcing Jack to let go of the shirt and also stumble backward a step. "I'm not your 'pal,' pal!"

Hale and Paul each grabbed Jack by one arm, not enough to restrain him if Jack made an effort, but enough to tell him that they would tighten their grip if it got out of hand.

"Please, this is improper." The voice was quiet and even-toned, but carried the weight of authority. It was, of course, President Moki's voice, and it had the desired effect: both Derek and Jack calmed down. Behind Derek, Jack noticed that Derek's two flunkies were releasing clenched fists.

The president continued: "These scientists have generously tried to help us. Regrettably, their effort was without result." He turned to Jack and Hale. "Fishing is the lifeblood of this island. I mustn't inflict unnecessary hardship on my people. And there simply isn't enough evidence for me to be absolutely certain that there is truly a danger in the waters. Unless and until such proof arrives, I shall lift the ban."

Derek's smile reminded Jack of the wolf in old cartoons that had just come up with a foolproof plan to trap the cartoon's hero. Sadly, Jack didn't have an anvil to drop on the fisherman's head as he said, "That's the spirit, Manny!"

Before Jack could say anything, Hale once again put

his hand on Jack's shoulder. "C'mon, Jack, I'll buy you a drink."

Jack didn't want a drink. Jack wanted to beat Derek Lawson to within an inch of his life. It was an odd feeling for a mild-mannered marine biologist who had harbored very few violent thoughts in his thirty-four years of life. But something about the New Zealander's smug arrogance brought out the worst in Jack.

It's not just that, though, he thought as he allowed Hale to steer him away from the pier and Derek's sneering face. *I had to stand by and watch while Diane died. I'll be damned if I'll let that happen again when it's something I can actually* help *with. Some kind of marine life killed Dak and those two women, I know it. And whatever it is will kill someone else unless we find out what it is.*

"Dad!" a voice cried.

Jack looked up to see Brandon running toward him. The boy was a mess, smeared with mud and dirt. For a brief instant, he saw Derek's face so covered in mud. *I should be so lucky*, Jack thought.

"I thought you'd never get here."

The last thing Jack needed right now was to listen to his son talk about what a great day he had exploring the island. "Not now, Brandon," he said through clenched teeth.

"You won't believe what I saw today!"

"I said, *not now*!" Jack snapped.

He and Hale continued into town. Jack needed that drink Hale offered if he was going to get the image of Derek Lawson out of his head.

For the second time that day, Brandon wandered aimlessly down the main beach of Malau. *I can't believe Dad yelled at me. Dad* never *yells at me.*

Something was wrong with Dad. Something serious. Brandon didn't know what to do.

He realized he was back at the spot where he saw that family having the picnic.

Mom.

Mom would know what to do. Whenever Dad got upset, Mom knew how to make him feel better. Mom always listened to Brandon, too.

He picked up a pebble and skimmed it into the ocean, but it only bounced once. *Great, here I am thinking I want my mommy.*

But he did. *I want Mom to be here so Dad won't yell at me.*

A shape washed up on the shore with the latest wave. Brandon looked down to see a wet, plastic disc. After a moment, he recognized it: the Frisbee that the guy with the dog threw into the ocean.

He picked it up and stared at it. Some lettering from the company that made it was written in a circle on one side.

I hate this place, Brandon decided. *People get killed here, and Dad goes off and does things without me, and people look at me like it's my fault that things are going wrong, and Dad gets angry for no reason, and Mom's not here and I* hate *it!*

He flung the Frisbee into the ocean as hard as he could.

The Frisbee flew into the night sky. Within seconds, Brandon couldn't see it anymore. He had no idea if it landed in the water or kept going on and on forever until it reached somewhere better.

Brandon wished someone would do that for him. He wished he really was Captain Marvel like he sometimes pretended. Captain Marvel could fly. Brandon wanted to be able to fly so he could go somewhere else. Like home. He wanted to go back to San Diego and be in a real school and not be Dad's stupid assistant or intern or whatever anymore.

Tears welled up in his eyes and he wiped them away. He was a big kid now, he *wouldn't* cry.

He turned and ran back to the hotel. He ran through the lobby, almost knocking over one of the bellhops. It took him a minute to fumble with the key before he got it open. He slammed the door shut behind him, put the camcorder down on the table between the laptops, and crawled into the bed near the window, not even bothering to put on his pajamas or wash up and brush his teeth or anything.

Only then did he allow himself to start crying.

He had no idea how much later it was that Dad came in. Brandon lay on his side so all Dad could see was his back. Brandon had been staring out the window at the beach and the night sky.

"We can talk now if you want," Dad said in a low voice.

Forget it, Brandon thought. *Let him think I'm asleep.* I *can ignore* him, *too*.

"Are you awake? Brandon?"

Nobody here but us sleeping kids.

After another minute, Brandon heard the door to the bathroom close. Then he closed his eyes and tried to sleep.

FOUR

In all his various travels, Jack Ellway had noticed that restaurants that served breakfast looked different when they did so than when they did for lunch or dinner. He couldn't really put his finger on what the difference was, but the morning meal suffused restaurants with a different atmosphere. *Brighter*, he thought, as he walked into Manny's the following morning. *Breakfast food's brighter colored anyhow, so it makes sense.*

He had been hoping to find Brandon. Unusually, Jack was up after his son; a typical morning had Jack trying every form of coercion he could think of to get Brandon out from under the covers, so for Brandon to be not only be up but gone had Jack worried. Not for the boy's safety; if he was worried about that, he wouldn't have left Brandon alone all day yesterday. No, what concerned Jack was how Brandon was feeling about his father right about now.

I can't believe I snapped at him like that. After a moment's thought: *Of course you believe it, stupid.*

You're always doing this, letting your feelings about work get in the way of things.

Diane always used to be the one to drag him back to earth when he got all swallowed up in his work, whether that work involved migration patterns or kelp forests or trying to find out why people were dying despite the best efforts of obnoxious fishermen.

He saw Alyson Hart sitting at the bar, a small plate of scrambled eggs and a glass of some kind of fruit juice in front of her. *Well, at least I'll get something out of this.* Alyson was nothing like Diane, which encouraged Jack. If she was like Diane, he'd have been suspicious of any attraction for her, figuring it to be his subconscious trying to find a Diane substitute. But this was a more legitimate attraction. *God knows what kind of social life an on-the-road marine biologist could possibly have, but it's good to know that the social muscles still work.*

Alyson saw his approach and smiled at him, showing perfect white teeth.

" 'Morning," she said.

"Hi," he said, sitting at the empty stool next to her. "Have you seen Brandon?"

"No. Are you worried?"

Jack sighed. He had tried to keep his tone neutral, but it obviously didn't work if the doctor could read his concern so easily. "Not worried, just…" He hesitated. "I was kind of abrupt with him last night." *Understatement #942,* he thought ruefully. "For him to be up and about so early this morning, he must be pretty pissed at me."

Before either of them could continue, the waitress—Tari, Jack remembered her name—appeared in front of them on the other side of the bar. "Breakfast?"

"Just coffee, please."

Tari nodded and turned to the coffeemaker behind her.

"It must be rough," Alyson said after a moment, "raising a child on your own."

Trying to sound nonchalant, Jack said, "It's only been a year. And we've been on the move the whole time. I figured it'd be the best thing for Brandon—keeping busy, new adventures, not having to dwell on…" Again, he hesitated. "You know, the bad stuff." *Christ, I sound like Brandon. What is it about this woman that ties my vocal cords up?* Tari placed a cup full of coffee in front of Jack, then moved both the cream pitcher and sugar bowl close to him—unnecessary, as it happened, since Jack drank his coffee black, but he appreciated the gesture and smiled at Tari.

Alyson took a sip of her juice before saying, slowly, "Best for Brandon, or best for you?"

"What're you talking about?" Jack asked, a trifle indignant.

Again she hesitated before slowly replying. "Running away," she started, then stopped.

"Running away?" Jack parroted, his indignance now more than a trifle.

"Never mind," Alyson said, looking down at her eggs in order to spear a forkful and shove it in her mouth.

"I guess you'd know all about running away, huh?" Jack said.

Alyson swallowed her eggs and fixed Jack with a steely gaze. "I would?"

"Yeah, this place is *crawling* with expatriates. I bet your story's a doozy."

The look Alyson gave him made Jack realize that he had screwed up royally for the second time in less than twenty-four hours.

"I'm not an expatriate," she said. "I grew up here. My father was the American liaison. After medical school, I came back home to run the clinic."

Not bad, he thought while sipping his coffee. *I spent yesterday cheesing off the entire fishing community on the island, followed it up by alienating my son, and now*

I've offended the local doctor. At this rate, I'll have the whole island out to lynch me by dawn tomorrow.

Aloud, he simply said, "Okay, I'm a jerk—sue me." He started to get up, leaving his coffee half-finished. He had a son to find, after all, and he had pretty much killed any chance of friendly relations with Alyson.

Then the young woman put her hand on his arm. "We were *both* being presumptuous," she said, her facial expression softer.

He looked at her, and she smiled. *God, that's a gorgeous smile.*

"We're even;" she said, "okay?"

Jack returned the smile but did not sit back down. "Okay." He took a final sip of the coffee, then placed a couple of dollars on the bar. "I'm gonna go look for Brandon."

"Good luck," Alyson said.

"Thanks."

As Jack approached the door, Hale walked in. "Jack, there you are. I've received satellite shots of the ocean floor. Thought you might like to take a look."

Jack blinked in surprise. "Uh, sure." He vaguely remembered a conversation the previous night over the third (or was it fourth?) beer. They were sitting in Rik's Bar and Grill, Hale still determined to continue their investigation. He had mentioned that his Institute had a satellite and he could get photos of the ocean floor.

"I thought your Institute was in Melbourne," Jack said as they walked toward Hale's bungalow. "How the hell did they get the photos to you so fast?"

Hale grinned. "What is it you yanks call it? The information superhighway? Magic of e-mail, mate—got 'em five minutes after they took 'em. Admittedly, the resolution's not as good in a JPEG file as it is in a proper print, but we'll have those by morning, and these'll do for now."

"Great," Jack said. *I can always talk to Brandon later.*

■ ■ ■

According to Paul Bateman, the big rock between the main beach and the small beach on Malau was called "Elephant Rock." Paul had told Brandon and Jack this over lunch, and also mentioned that it was a great place to gather up slow-moving sea life.

That's what brought Brandon to the rock that morning.

Brandon saw a few mud crabs and mollusks. *Perfect.* He grabbed them and dropped them in the small bucket he'd picked up at one of the small stands on the outskirts of the beach.

He spent the better part of the morning gathering up various invertebrate sea life until he felt he had enough. Then he headed back toward the jungle. *Just gotta hope that the little guy's still there.*

Mom had always said that the world was always brighter after a good night's sleep. Once he got older, Brandon realized that she only said that to convince him to go to bed at eight o'clock, but today he saw that she was right. He woke up bright and early, determined to befriend the small creature he'd met the day before. *Dad doesn't want to take me along on things, he wants to yell at me—well, fine. Let him. I've got a new friend.*

Finding the lagoon again proved pretty easy—the jungle was small enough that Brandon was amazed it even had a lagoon, to be honest.

He sat himself down on the wet bank at the edge of the lagoon and waited.

After a few minutes, he shifted in the sand, wondering if his hunch was wrong.

Just as he was about to give up and head back to the hotel, the water started to ripple. Muttering "Shazam," with a smile, he watched as the salamander-thingie poked its head out of the water. It looked at Brandon with those big eyes, then climbed out of the water and stood on its hind legs again.

This is so cool, Brandon thought. He was practically

nose to nose with the little guy, and this time it didn't run away—it just stared back at him.

"I bet you haven't had breakfast," Brandon said. He pulled the mollusks and mud crabs out of the bucket and laid them out on the edge of the lagoon like it was a buffet table.

It stared down at the fish like it had no idea what they were. Then it fixed its gaze back on Brandon.

When he was six, Brandon had wanted a dog more than anything else in the world. He begged and pleaded with Mom and Dad until finally they gave in at Christmas and got him a puppy. Brandon had named him Casey, and he loved the dog more than anything in the world. Dad had built a dog run in the back of the house in San Diego, and Brandon would spend hours there with Casey.

It broke his heart a year and a half later when Brandon went out to find a hole in the dog run's fence and no sign of Casey. They spent weeks searching for him, putting HAVE YOU SEEN THIS DOG? signs all over the neighborhood, but they never found him.

Years later, the thing Brandon remembered most about Casey was that he ate like a pig. He ate constantly, and he always ambled up to Brandon with his big blue eyes all soulful and an expectant look on his face.

The little guy had that look on its face right now. On the spot, Brandon decided to name it Casey, too.

So why the hell isn't Casey going for the food? "C'mon," he said, "they're mollusks and mud crabs. *Invertebrates.* That's what salamanders eat."

Apparently, nobody bothered to tell Casey this, because it was very obviously still hungry, and just as obviously uninterested in the fish.

Great. What do I do now? I suppose I could ask Dad, he thought, then dismissed it. He didn't want to talk to Dad yet.

So he'd just have to find out for himself.

"I'll be back, okay?" he said.

Casey actually made a noise at that—it almost sounded like a whine. *Do salamanders whine?*

No, he thought, *but salamanders walk on four legs and eat invertebrates. So fat lot of good that does me.*

He left the fish behind in case Casey changed its mind, grabbed the bucket, and ran back toward the beach and the hotel room. Maybe if he surfed the net and checked through Dad's books, he could find something.

Ba-da-doom, da-doom. Ba-da-doom, da-doom.

This was the moment Nat lived for. The beach, the surf, the two gorgeous women dancing, the bonfire, the sunset—all of it faded. There was just Nat, the stool he sat on, and the bongo drums anchored between his legs.

Ba-da-doom, da-doom. Ba-da-doom, da-doom.

It was just the pounding rhythm. The feel of the skins against his calloused hands. The beat matching time with the pounding of blood through his heart.

Ba-da-doom, da-doom. Ba-da-doom, da-doom.

The spell was inevitably broken—this time by Don next to him crying out, "Whoooooooooo!" as the beat intensified. Nat sighed, but kept pounding away on the two linked drums wedged between his knees.

Ba-da-doom, da-doom. Ba-da-doom, da-doom.

Those all-too-brief moments of percussional satori were what Nat lived for. Don's scream brought Nat back to other concerns besides the pureness of the beat: to Don and Keith next to him on the conga and doumbek, respectively; to Mira and Jan dancing in the sand in front of them, Mira rattling a tambourine to add a little spice to the beat; to the group of Australian teenagers sitting around a bonfire; to the woman and the little girl playing catch with a red and white beach ball; and to Dak.

Ba-da-doom, da-doom. Ba-da-doom, da-doom.

Dak was the real reason they were here. True, jam ses-

sions among Malau's percussionists weren't exactly
uncommon, but this one had a purpose—it was Dak's
memorial. Sure, there was a funeral at St. Theresa's, but
as far as Nat, Don, and Keith were concerned, that was
for the civilians. Tonight, Dak's fellow musicians would
celebrate his life and commiserate over his death in proper fashion: with an all-night jam session. That's what he
would have wanted.

Ba-da-doom, da-doom. Ba-da-doom, da-doom.

Still no sign of Kulani. Nat hadn't entirely expected
Kulani to show up, since it involved coming to the ocean.
Nat had a feeling that Lani wouldn't be getting too close
to the water for a while yet. But not having Dak's fiancée
here took something away from the proceedings.

Ba-da-doom, da-doom. Ba-da-doom, da-doom.

Nat took a quick glance out onto the ocean. It seemed
to be more turbulent than usual tonight—the waves were
a bit choppier, even though there was little wind. *Maybe
it's 'cause of all those damn quakes*, Nat thought, and
turned back to keep an eye on Don and Keith.

Ba-da-doom, da-doom. Ba-da-doom, da-doom.

The beat started to modulate as Don decided to try
something fancier on the conga. Nat grinned and followed along.

Ba-da-doom, da-doom. Ba-da-doom, da-doom.

At one point in her dance, Mira turned so that she was
facing Nat, and their eyes locked. She winked at him. Nat
actually missed a beat, he was so surprised, and it took
him a couple of measures to bring himself back in line
with the others. Neither Don nor Keith seemed to notice,
and they certainly didn't complain—it was just a jam session, after all, where perfection was not a necessity—but
Nat's head reeled. He thought Mira had a thing going
with that fisherman from New Zealand that was always
hanging out at Manny's.

Ba-da-doom, da-doom. Ba-da-doom, da-POW!

Nat looked up sharply at the noise, which did a lot more to throw the trio off than Mira's wink.

He couldn't quite bring himself to believe what he saw.

Standing in the shallow end of the surf, wave water pooling around its legs, was something that looked like a really big lizard. Nat figured it was at least nine or ten feet tall, and it had dark green scaly skin. Little horn-like things ran up and down its back, with two more pronounced ones on top of its head. Standing on its hind legs, its clawed forelegs—hands? claws?—had shards of beach ball in them. In addition to this, the woman and girl who were playing catch with the beach ball were now screaming and running. *Jesus, did the thing try to join in the game of catch, or what?*

A scream right in his ear brought Nat to the realization that perhaps he should follow the lead of the woman and girl and get his ass off the beach. Grabbing the metal struts of the bongo set, he got up and, abandoning the stool, started running.

Still, he couldn't help but look back to see what the big lizard was doing. To Nat's amazement, it too was running—it seemed to be pursuing the little girl. It alighted on top of a jeep.

"Aw, *no*," came a voice from Nat's left. The voice belonged to Don, and after a moment, Nat remembered that the jeep belonged to him, too.

Nat continued running, giving the jeep a wide berth. As he passed it, he saw the little girl trip and fall, her small legs unable to navigate the rocky sand.

Fear gripped Nat as he saw the big lizard leap off of Don's jeep right toward the girl, looking for all the world like a huge cat about to take on a helpless mouse.

A woman screamed, *"Nooooo!"* Nat saw that it was the woman who had been playing catch with the girl— her mother?

Why am I still watching this? Nat wondered. He had stopped running, transfixed by this gruesome tableau. Keith, Mira, and Jan had all disappeared—even Don hadn't stuck around to look after his jeep. And then, to his surprise, Nat found himself running *toward* the creature, the image of himself whacking the big lizard with his bongos in his mind.

Before rational thought even had a chance to take over—or at least to talk sense into someone determined to face a large monster armed only with percussion—a man leapt out of nowhere with a body board and slammed it into the creature's side.

The lizard screamed. Nat didn't think lizards *could* scream—but then, he didn't think lizards could grow to be so tall, walk on their hind legs, and shred innocent beach balls, either.

Then the thing turned and slashed at the body board. The board's wielder, for his part, seemed content to drop it and dash for the little girl. He picked her up in one fluid motion under one arm and ran toward the screaming woman. Grabbing her hand with his other arm, the three of them ran off.

People were now running around like crazy all over the beach, screaming, yelling, and generally making a lot of noise. Nat couldn't figure out why he wasn't one of them. Instead he just stared at the big lizard.

The lizard shook its head, then turned toward Nat.

Nat blinked, as if coming out of a trance.

Yikes. He turned and ran away, as fast as his legs could carry him, the weight of the bongos barely slowing him down.

A couple of hours spent surfing a variety of salamander and newt sites on the World Wide Web led Brandon to the conclusion that he had the right idea, but didn't provide enough of a menu for Casey. The food of choice for this type of amphibious life seemed to be bugs: pillbugs, beetles, earthworms, small millipedes, insects, aphids, small moths, and other night-flying insects.

Well, I sure ain't gonna wait until night, but I should be able to gather up something. With a smile of satisfaction, Brandon shut down the laptop, unhooked the modem from the jack, gathered up a few of Dad's sample jars, and went out in search of insect life.

By dusk, he had a good selection. He then stopped at Manny's to ask for a strip of raw beef. Tari looked at him like he had two heads, but Brandon explained that it was for an experiment he and his father were running. Shrugging, Tari went into the kitchen, had a lengthy conversation with the cook, and liberated a strip of beef for Brandon. She didn't even charge him for it, though she did admonish him not to tell Manny.

The sites he found all recommended waving a piece of raw meat to attract the salamander. Admittedly, that might not be necessary in this case. For one thing, Casey seemed to respond directly to Brandon's presence. More to the point, Brandon was really shooting in the dark generally here—he thought of Casey as an overgrown salamander only by default, since that was the closest analogue he could come up with in his own experience. And just because it had a resemblance to salamanders didn't mean it would act like one.

But he had to try.

So he ventured back to the lagoon. He arrived to find that the mollusks and mud crabs lay untouched; no sign of Casey.

As Brandon took the strip of meat out, though, Casey's head popped up from the water. It—*no, "he," if you're gonna name the little guy after Casey, he's a he, not an it*—approached the shore once again.

Brandon moved to upend the sample jars, but before he could, Casey stopped and looked around, as if responding to something.

"What's up, little guy? What're you seeing?" Brandon asked. He looked around also, but aside from a light mist that had been rising in the jungle since the sun started to go down, he didn't see anything. There wasn't a breeze at the moment, so the trees didn't even sway.

Casey's head jerked, as if he'd heard a noise. "What're you hearing?" Brandon asked.

Then Casey let out another whine—longer, louder, and higher-pitched than the one he'd uttered after refusing Brandon's fish breakfast.

What the heck is he reacting to?

Paul Bateman saw Jack Ellway and Ralph Hale walking toward Manny's. Paul himself was also headed that way, having spent the afternoon developing pictures and dictating notes into his handheld tape recorder. He smiled at the sight of the two scientists, as one of the notes he'd made to himself was, *Talk to Ellway and Hale about what they saw yesterday and today and pick their brains regarding what killed Dak.*

"Howdy there, fellas," he said as he caught up to them. "So, what news from our visiting scientific dignitaries?"

Hale snorted.

Jack said, "Not a lot, unfortunately. Doctor Hale did get some satellite photos."

"Really?" Paul said, intrigued.

"Yeah, but they didn't really help much. I mean, they confirmed some of my theories about how the seismic activity would affect the local marine life—but as for explaining what happened to Dak..." He trailed off.

"So, do you think—"

Before Paul could finish his question, people started running through the streets. *What the hell's going on?*

The people were all coming from the beach, Paul realized. Immediately, he checked the camera that hung from a strap around his neck, made sure that it was loaded and ready to go. Then one person literally crashed into him, knocking him over.

Whoever it was, they didn't even slow down to see if Paul was okay. Jack and Hale helped him up. "You okay?"

Paul nodded as he grabbed the two men's wrists and got to his feet. He listened to the various voices of the panicky people around him.

"—big lizard—"

"—out of the water—"

"—almost killed that little girl—"

"—hind legs—"

"—like, nine feet tall, man—"

"—anybody got a gun—"

"—it's bloody *huge*—"

"—gotta kill that thing—"

"—seen Manny or Joe?"

Jack and Hale exchanged a glance, then ran toward the beach, fighting against the stream of people. Paul, knowing a good story when he saw one, followed in their wake.

They got to the edge of the beach just in time to see a massive form moving toward the jungle. It looked for all the world like a nine-foot-tall lizard running on its hind legs.

It took Paul a moment to realize that it really *was* a nine-foot-tall lizard running on its hind legs.

That's impossible. Big scaly monsters don't exist outside of movies.

He blinked, rubbed his eyes, and looked again.

The lizard had the permanent forward lean common to amphibians, like it was expecting to have to move on all fours any second. Covered in dark green scales, it also had a series of tiny horns running up and down its back and tail, culminating in two not-so-tiny horns on top of its head—a big one right above the bridge of its nose, and another, smaller one right behind that.

It reared its head back and let out a sound that could have been a scream, or maybe a moan. *Right, like I'm going to judge the emotional state of a nine-foot-tall lizard.*

Paul noticed two of Joe Movita's cops—Mal and Jimmy—going in after it on scooters, each of them armed with rifles.

"No, for God's sake, don't kill it!" That was Jack, screaming at the two cops who, for their part, were ignoring him, though they hadn't started shooting yet, either. This didn't surprise Paul—both cops were part of a weekly poker game that Paul also participated in, and they were both quite proud of the fact that they'd served as police officers for as long as they had without ever discharging a weapon outside of the firing range.

"Where'd you store your gear, Jack?" Hale asked.

"Over here," Jack said, running toward a small shack about thirty feet in the other direction down the beach.

Paul and Hale followed behind the marine biologist. "What's he got that'll help?" Paul asked.

"Tranq gun," Hale said.

Jack ran inside the shack. By the time Paul and Hale joined him, he had thrown open the lid of one of the crates and was loading darts into a huge rifle.

Paul had finally gotten over the shock and accepted the fact that, yes, a giant monster was loose on the island. This was news. In his head, he started laying out the multi-page coverage of the lizard's attack for his special edition of the *Weekly News*. He also finally remembered the camera around his neck—bringing the camera to his eye, he ran off several shots of Jack loading the rifle.

Ignoring Paul, Jack finished loading, then turned to Hale. "C'mon."

As they got back outside, rain started pouring down. *Heck of a time for a storm*, Paul thought, annoyed. The rain would only serve to muck up his pictures.

The three of them ran toward the jungle. Chief Movita was approaching the jungle in his jeep, siren blazing.

"Chief," Jack cried out, catching up with Joe's jeep, "we can't kill this thing, it's—"

"Excuse me?" the chief interrupted, putting on the brakes and sparing an annoyed glance at Jack's rifle. "This is not a good place for a civilian—"

"I have tranquilizer darts, Chief. I can bring it down unharmed."

Joe seemed to consider this, then: "All right, Ellway, I'll give you a *chance*, but if you can't bring that sucker down, we will. Hop in."

Jack, Hale, and Paul all clambered into the jeep. Before Paul even had a chance to settle into his seat, Joe took off into the jungle.

Paul once again started taking pictures—he wanted to get the verdant atmosphere of the jungle in the shots from here on in; the rain would fog the images a bit, but also make it even more atmospheric. *Of course, there's a limit as to how atmospheric I can get in black and white on newsprint. Wonder how much Kal would charge for color?*

It wasn't hard to figure out the creature's path—ninefoot-tall lizards didn't exactly move with subtlety. Paul didn't know a lot about animals in general—he spent most of his time in biology class drawing moustaches on the pictures of sperm—but he was pretty sure that lizards that size were *not* found in nature.

Besides, the thing was wailing like a banshee. *It almost sounds afraid.*

As soon as the jeep was close enough, Jack aimed the rifle and fired.

The dart struck the lizard in the left leg.

It didn't even slow the thing down.

Paul cursed as he snapped picture after picture—he only had about ten exposures left and his spare film was back at the office.

Jack shot a few more darts at the lizard, and this time it did slow down—and screamed.

When he was eleven, Paul's father took him on a trip into Sequoia National Park. While hiking amidst the massive redwoods, he heard a scream like what the lizard had just uttered. It was a dog that had been trapped under a huge branch. The branch—which had the thickness of a small maple tree trunk—had apparently fallen from one of the trees. The dog was unfortunate not to have been killed instantly. Instead, its legs had been shattered.

For the rest of the trip, Paul heard that dog's cry in his dreams. But he got over it soon enough.

Now, over a decade later, he remembered that dog as the lizard cried in an almost identical manner.

Shaking off the memories, Paul peered back into the viewfinder. The lizard had backed up against a large tree, and was thrashing about. Paul snapped another picture—

—just as Jimmy got too close on his scooter. Three pictures in Paul's roll chronicled the creature pulling one of its forelegs—no, *arms*—into a backhand motion; the arm slashing through the air right at Jimmy's chest; and finally, Jimmy being thrown from his vehicle, blood flying in all directions from his thorax as the backhand sweep finished its arc.

Stunned, Paul kept snapping photos, but now he was on autopilot. He just kept his lens aimed at the creature as Jack fired dart after dart into it.

Just as the chief said, "Okay, that's it, move in," the creature gave out another yell and—with a dozen tranq darts protruding from its scaly hide—fell to the ground with an impact that rivaled the recent tremors.

Paul hopped out of the jeep and moved in closer, as did Jack, the chief, and Mal.

Suddenly, the creature reared its head and tail, and Paul leapt back involuntarily, his finger brushing against the camera button.

The creature fell again to the ground, its beady eyes now closed. Paul sighed—the last picture in the roll would probably be of the top of one of the trees.

Chief Movita ran toward Jimmy and knelt down beside him. "Mal, get Doctor Hart in here *now*."

Mal nodded and dashed off.

The chief looked up angrily at Jack. "So glad you were able to bring it down unharmed."

"I—" Jack started.

"Save it," Joe said, rising and walking away.

Hale put his hand on Jack's shoulder. "You did the right thing, mate. Now we can study the thing properly."

"Yeah," Jack said. Paul wondered what was going through the marine biologist's head.

Before anything else could happen, Brandon popped out from behind one of the bushes, crying, "Dad!" Paul blinked in surprise. Jack had been looking for his son all day. He and Hale had come into Paul's office in search of Brandon that morning, but Paul hadn't seen him. When Paul went to lunch at Manny's, Tari said that Brandon had been in earlier, but she had no idea where the boy was at that point.

"Brandon?" Jack said. "What're you doing here?"

"Uh, I, ah, saw everyone was running in here, so I wanted to see what happened."

The kid's lying, Paul thought without hesitation. He

knew that guilty look—he had it himself as a twelve-year-old when he lied to his parents.

Based on the look on Jack's face, the lie had gone as far over his head as Paul's had to his parents. He seemed completely accepting of what Brandon said. *Interesting— wonder what the kid's been doing.*

Brandon looked over at the prone creature. "What *is* that thing?"

Jack pulled his son into an embrace. "You shouldn't've come in here, Brandon, it was dangerous."

"I'm sorry, Dad, I didn't—I mean—"

"It's okay," Jack said, breaking the hug. "To answer your question, I have no idea what it is. What say we try to figure it out together?" He smiled.

Brandon nodded, and smiled back.

Well, they're all one big happy family again, Paul thought as he rewound the film in his camera, *but what about tall, green, and scary here?*

FIVE

Derek Lawson had to admit that it was a good setup. At the direction of Hale and that American jackass Ellway, they had set up an oversized shark cage to house that thing they had captured the night before. It was hooked up to the pier and rigged it with buoys in such a way that it was part underwater, part above water.

Derek stood with Kikko, Naru, and a bunch of other people near the pier. The three of them had missed the excitement, sadly. They were washing down the trawler—a Japanese tourist that they had taken on a fishing jaunt proved more prone to seasickness than she thought she would be—and by the time they found out that a nine-foot lizard was on the loose, it had already been brought down.

Derek shook his head and looked at Kikko. "Thought I'd seen everything the sea could chuck up, but that thing is un-bloody-believable."

"What do you think they'll do with it?"

"Turn it into cash for themselves, most like," Derek said with a snort.

They were held back about twenty feet from the pier by Marc and Mal, two of the local cops. Derek didn't know why they bothered. While everyone wanted to see it, nobody really wanted to get all that close to it.

Of course, Derek noticed that Ellway wasn't forced to stay back. He and Bateman were crouched on the pier next to the cage. Bateman's presence made sense, him being Malau's only real press and all, but what the hell was Ellway doing there? How did he rate?

He voiced this question aloud to Marc, who said, "He's the expert—he's, y'know, a marine biologist. 'Sides, he's the one that brought the sucker down."

Derek noticed Manny and Chief Movita coming through the police barricade, along with Hale and Ellway's snot-nosed kid. *Great, more bleedin' outsiders getting special privileges. What the hell's this island coming to, anyhow?*

He then fixed his gaze back on the caged lizard.

What a magnificent creature it is, he thought. *I could make a bundle off that thing.* He smiled. The latest in a long line of fishermen from Matakana, New Zealand, Derek Lawson had relocated to Malau after a particularly messy divorce proceeding that resulted in his being required to make alimony payments that he had neither the interest nor the ability to make. Malau was sufficiently far away from Matakana that he didn't have to worry about paying that witch Lucille, nor have to deal with those taxes he hadn't gotten around to.

Besides, here he got a certain amount of respect. In Matakana, he was just one of dozens of fishers. In Malau, he stood out.

But now maybe it was time to move on to something better. He and Kikko and Naru had been talking for years about making enough money to open a restaurant on Fiji, but the honest truth was that they'd never manage it. Lawson Fishing Inc. did well enough to earn all three of them a living, but every time they thought they'd saved enough, some major repair to the boat would come up, or their taxes would be raised, or revenues would start slowing down, or the equipment would need to be replaced, or *something*.

Right now, Malau was one of the South Seas' better-kept secrets. It hadn't become the major tourist attraction that other locales had become, rather remaining the favorite vacation spot of a comparatively small number of people from around the world. That kept the place a lot more civilized than most, but it also was one reason why Derek and the others would never have the kind of money they needed to implement the Fiji dream.

Maybe it's about time I change that, Derek thought. *Make people start talking about Malau in the same breath that they talk about Fiji or Kalor or Tahiti. And make enough cash so that I can pay off the taxes and get that witch off my back. Maybe even open that restaurant some day down the line.*

The key, he knew, was that big lizard.

He saw Doctor Hart approach the ever-growing collection of folks near the lizard, and Derek decided that, if they deserved a closer look, then dammit, so did he. He sidled up to Marc and whispered, "Hey, Marc, mind if I get a closer look at the thing?"

"C'mon, Derek, you know the rules. Everyone except—"

"Y'know, your kid's been talkin' about fishin' lessons."

Marc frowned. "How'd you know about that?"

Derek shrugged. "He asked me. Wanted to know how much the lessons'd cost."

Marc shook his head. "I told him we couldn't afford it. I don't want—"

"You can afford it if it's free," he said. "All you gotta do is let me in closer." He smiled. "C'mon, Marc, lemme get a gander at the thing. For the kid. Hm?"

Marc stared at Derek for a minute, then sighed. "All right—but none of your bullshit, Derek. *Free* lessons, no 'extras,' got it?"

"My word of honor, mate," Derek said with a grin as he walked toward the pier.

Paul Bateman had to admit, he was enjoying watching Jack fawn over the monster he had captured.

Not that there was much to fawn over just at the moment. The creature was still somewhat groggy from the tranquilizers—it seemed to be moving in slow motion compared to the frightening speed with which it had ambulated the previous night. Paul had already taken several photographs of the thing in captivity, as well as a bunch while Hale and Ellway supervised the placing of the monster in the cage last night. If he spent the afternoon writing up the articles and developing the pictures, he figured his special big-lizard edition of the *Weekly News* would be out by tomorrow morning, if Kal came through.

Of course, the primary question the monster's presence raised was the same one that everyone on Malau had been asking for two days, one it behooved Paul to make the focus of his coverage. So he asked Jack, "Do you think this is what killed Dak and the two tourist girls?"

"Probably," Jack said. "I took a cast of its claws and teeth for Alyson to compare to Dak's body. She'll do that when she has a minute."

Paul nodded. Alyson's first priority was treating Jimmy and the people who were injured on the beach. There certainly wasn't a rush on checking the casts—it's not like the monster was going anywhere.

"In any case," Jack continued, standing upright, "the

big guy here is certainly strong enough. I fired enough tranquilizer darts to knock out a killer whale. Of course, its metabolism could be unbelievably slow—or its blood vessels constricted."

Also standing upright, and grinning, Paul said, "Or maybe it's just one tough mother."

Returning the grin, Jack said, "Right." He turned back to the creature. "Beautiful coloring, for a male. Superficially, it looks like a member of the order *urodela*—which includes about three hundred different species of salamanders."

Paul was startled by an Australian-accented voice from behind him, "How the hell did it get so *big*?" He turned to see Hale, along with Manny, Joe, and Brandon, approaching them from behind.

Jack, for his part, didn't seem at all startled, but simply answered the question: "There are salamanders that reach a length of six feet—but they're exclusively aquatic. Terrestrial salamanders, or amphibious ones like this thing, are rarely longer than a few inches—and none has ever been observed walking on its hind legs, which is what makes this thing so unique."

"And dangerous," Joe added.

Paul sighed. *Leave it to the chief to find the cloud in the silver lining.*

Jack looked like he was about to reply, but Manny came to the diplomatic rescue before the marine biologist had a chance to put his foot in it. "This poor creature does not seem capable of much harm at the moment."

Jack seemed content with that answer, and turned his attention back to the lizard. The chief, for his part, still looked angry, but said nothing more. Paul couldn't entirely blame him, though the latest word was that Jimmy would survive. *Still, as far as he's concerned, the only thing that matters is that the big guy mauled one of his men.*

Brandon wandered closer to the cage, standing next to his father and in front of Paul. "Can't you just turn him loose? Maybe he'll go home."

Paul blinked in surprise at the question. *Brandon hadn't struck me as being that naïve before.*

"Maybe he can't go home," Jack said. "Maybe he came onto the island because he was having trouble surviving. We've never seen anything like him. He might be the last of his species—or one of a kind."

"What if—" Brandon hesitated. "What if he *isn't* one of a kind? What if, like, another one came along? Then would you let 'em go?"

Jack shook his head. "No. Certainly not right away. I wouldn't be much of a scientist if I did *that*, Brandon. C'mon, you know the drill as well as I do. We'd need to find out what they are and where they come from." He smiled. "If it's a new species, maybe I can name it after you: a Brandonomadon."

That got a rise out of the kid, and he, too, smiled. Paul, though, was curious as to why Brandon was asking these questions—especially in light of what he said, and didn't say, the previous night in the jungle. *Methinks the boy knows more than he's saying*, Paul thought. *Of course, it could just be twelve-year-old weirdness. Still, I'd better keep an eye on him.*

"That day," Brandon said, "what I was trying to tell you—"

"If there are *more* of these monsters," Joe interrupted, having listened in on the conversation, "we must prepare a defense."

Brandon whirled on the chief. "What does that mean? Does that mean you'd kill 'em?" The boy sounded anguished, like Joe was talking about murdering the kid's pet cat or something.

Joe had the good grace to soften his expression when he replied, "I would do what was necessary for public safety."

"Dad," Brandon said, turning back to his father, "you wouldn't let 'em be killed, would you?"

Jack hesitated, and spoke very slowly. "I'd do everything I could to prevent it. But it might be beyond my control."

Just then, Alyson approached. Paul took the fact that she had the time to leave the clinic as a good sign.

"How's Jimmy, Doctor?" Joe asked.

"He'll survive. He's lost a lot of blood, but we had plenty of B-positive on hand, and a few donors for back-up. I wouldn't put him back on duty for a couple of weeks, but he should recover."

"Good," Joe said, with a pointed look at Jack.

"The others," Alyson continued, "have only minor cuts and scrapes." She turned to Jack. "I shipped the casts off to Kalor, so they can check it against Dak. I don't have the equipment for a proper comparison here, though my gut tells me it'll be a match."

Alyson then looked down at Brandon, who, Paul noticed, looked a bit distressed. *All this forensic-evidence talk can't be good for a twelve-year-old*, Paul thought. *Then again, when I was twelve, I would've thought it was cool, so what do I know?*

"You okay, Brandon?" Alyson asked with what Paul, to his surprise, would swear was a maternal tone.

"I'm okay," the boy assured her.

"I been thinking," said a voice from behind Paul. He turned to see Derek Lawson approaching the cage. *Christ on a crutch, what did we do to deserve this? I thought the chief's guys were supposed to keep the riffraff away from the lizard.*

Derek continued: "We could build a nice little enclosure right over there." He pointed to a spot near the pier on the edge of the beach. "Charge five dollars for adults, children under twelve half-price..."

I don't believe this, Paul thought. *He's already got the amusement park built in his head. "Big-Lizard Land."*

Jack looked at Derek with something like revulsion. "A freak show isn't really what I had in mind."

Derek laughed derisively. "What *you* had in mind? It's all about you again, innit, mate?"

"Look," Jack said angrily, "no freak show. Got it?"

Paul had only known Jack Ellway for a couple of days, but the impression he had gotten was of an even-tempered, if occasionally absent-minded, man. He'd only gotten angry twice that Paul had seen—both times at the instigation of Derek Lawson. *That's our boy*, he thought, *always bringing out the best in people.*

For his part, Derek turned to Manny. "What's going on here, mates? The creature wandered onto our island. We should be calling the shots."

"Putting it in your terms, Derek," Paul said, "Jack's the guy who bagged the thing. He's got the claim. Kinda like that huge swordfish you got last year that you insisted on hanging on your wall instead of selling to Manny."

If Derek had a reaction to Paul's dig, he didn't show it, much to Paul's disappointment. Instead, the fisherman turned to the president. "C'mon, Manny, exercise some authority. Think about tourism."

Manny was his usual phlegmatic self as he calmly responded. "I shall exercise *moral* authority and think of this creature and what is best for the people of this island. As long as public safety is not an issue, I will defer to the scientists."

This time, Derek's facial expression did change—to one of disgust. He turned and walked off, pausing to crouch down on the pier next to the cage. "I could've made you famous."

Then—in one of those moments that Paul would spend the rest of his life regretting that it happened too fast for him to capture it on film—the lizard made a lunge toward Derek, crashing futilely against the bars of the cage.

Derek jumped back, startled, tried to stand up, lost his balance, and fell backward off the pier and into the ocean.

Joe, kind-hearted person that he was, went over to help Derek out of the water, to the tune of the laughter of the assembled multitudes. Not surprisingly, Derek refused the help, clambering out of the shallow water on his own and stomping off toward his trawler, on which he also lived.

"By the way, Jack," Hale said after everyone's guffaws at Derek's expense had died down, "I got those satellite prints in from the Institute. Now that we got somethin' a little better to go on…" He trailed off.

"Right," Jack said.

The wheels started turning in Paul's head. "Listen, Jack, I was hoping to talk to you guys about this for the special edition of the paper I'm doing." *Now he's going to tell me that he and Hale are too busy.*

"I'm sorry Paul, but Doctor Hale and I have a lot of work to do, and—"

Paul held up a hand. "It's okay, I kinda figured that. How's about I talk to Brandon instead?" He turned to the boy. "It'll give you a chance to see how an actual newspaper works."

Hale grinned. "How an actual small-town newspaper run by one bloke works, anyhow."

Shrugging, Paul said, "Well, yeah. And it'll give me a chance to get some factoids for the paper without disturbing your Dad from his work."

"Whaddaya say, Brandon?" Jack said. "This is the sort of thing scientists tend to fob off on their assistants anyhow."

Brandon smiled. "Yeah, okay."

"Great," Paul said. *And maybe I can find out just what, if anything, the kid's hiding.* He indicated the way toward town. "Shall we?"

"Yeah, okay," Brandon repeated.

"I'll come get you in a couple of hours, Brandon," Jack said.

Brandon nodded as Paul led the boy away from the pier and in the direction of the *Malau Weekly News* offices.

The small wooden building that housed Paul's newspaper used to be the local dive shop. Surrounded by trees and off the main road, the owners of the dive shop had decided to move to a more visible locale, leaving the space available. Initially, Paul had also lived in the small building, until the *Weekly News*'s revenues were at the point where he could afford his own place.

He unlocked the front door and led Brandon in. Paul grabbed a tape recorder and started asking Brandon a few technical questions about what the Ellways did generally.

"Didn't you ask us this stuff at lunch the other day?"

Paul smiled. "Yeah, but I didn't have my tape recorder then."

"Okay," Brandon said, and proceeded to answer all of Paul's questions by rote. *The kid knows this stuff pretty well*, Paul thought. *Either that, or he's real good at making it up and sounding convincing.*

As they talked, Paul took Brandon into the dark room and gave the kid a crash course in picture developing. Brandon expressed surprise at how low-tech it all was, but Paul just shrugged and said that some things didn't require high-tech.

They talked for a few hours, first about his and Jack's work in general, then about some of the other trips they'd taken together in the last year. Paul avoided the subject of Brandon's mother, which he assumed to be a sensitive subject. By the time he had selected and made prints of the captured monster, they had moved on to talking about the events of the last couple of days.

"Do you think Derek's gonna get to do what he wants?" Brandon asked.

"Not too likely," Paul said. "Derek still labors under the delusion that people respect him. He's got great fishing instincts, and his catches are generally worth it, but as a person, he's regarded somewhere below the plankton."

Brandon laughed at that. "I guess. What about what Dad said?"

Paul frowned. "What do you mean?"

"If there was more than one of these guys around, what do you think would happen?"

Paul thought about that for a moment, looking down at the print of the nine-foot lizard. *God*, he thought, *imagine a whole family of these things*.

"Well," he finally said, "I'd say that whenever humanity has power over nature, nature's usually the big loser."

Brandon sat quietly for a moment after Paul said that. *The kid knows something*. "Why do you ask?"

"I'm just curious," he said much too quickly. "I mean, the police chief kept talking about how he might have to kill it."

"Well, the thing *is* responsible for three deaths, Brandon. I mean, when a dog gets rabid and is in danger of hurting people, they shoot it. Our Ghidrah lookalike out there has already proven to be dangerous. They may not have a choice."

"Ghidrah?" Brandon asked, sounding confused.

Paul smiled. "Old Japanese monster movie."

"Oh." Brandon looked over at Paul's computer. "So what do you do with the pictures, paste 'em up?"

"Thank God, no," Paul said, noting that Brandon had quickly changed the subject. "I used to before I could afford the upgrade, but I do it all on the computer now."

I won't push now, Brandon, but you know something, and I'm gonna find out what it is.

In the bungalow Ralph Hale had rented, Jack watched as the older man spread a large map of the area, a smaller topographical map that included geological referents, and several satellite photos on his dining room table. The previous contents of the table—piles of papers and books, mostly—had been dumped unceremoniously on the floor. At once, Jack noticed that the resolution on the satellite photos was of much greater quality on the prints than they were on the JPEG computer files he and Hale had looked at the previous day. There were also several photos he didn't recognize.

"What's with the extras?"

"My techies at the Institute came through for me," Hale said with a grin. "They got their hands on some shots taken by the Topex Satellite over the last couple of months. So, what're we looking for?"

"Well," Jack said, "salamanders aren't all that common around these parts, but the most likely breeding ground for aquatic salamanders would be a submerged mountain range—" he peered at the topographical map "—like that one." He pointed to an undersea strip labelled IOZIMA RIDGE that, relative to Malau, ran northeastward into the Pacific Ocean.

Hale peered at the map. "That ridge runs for two thousand miles." He looked up at Jack. "Uninterrupted."

Nodding, Jack said, "Which would explain why no one's spotted our creature or any like it."

As Jack spoke, Hale started rummaging through the satellite photos. "C'mon," he muttered, "where is it? A-ha!" He liberated first one, then a second photo from the pile and laid them out side by side over the map. "Look at this, Jack." He pointed to the one on the left. It provided an image that matched the basic structure shown on the geographical map of the westernmost part of the Iozima Ridge, but had the darker, negative-image–type look of most satellite photos. "Here's the ridge at its closest proximity to Malau. Topex took this shot last month." He pointed to the photo on the right, which was superficially similar, but for the Hale Institute logo on the edge—and the hairline across one part of the ridge, which Hale ran his finger down. "This little artery wasn't there a month ago. I suspect it's a fault line created by all the recent seismic activity. It leads directly from the ridge to the shallow waters off Malau."

Jack frowned. "Kinda like an expressway that's suddenly developed an off-ramp."

Hale laughed. "Whoa, Jack, these technical terms are makin' me dizzy."

Returning the laugh, Jack said, "Sorry—force of habit when your assistant is twelve." He shifted the photos and looked again at the map. "I wonder if our amphibian friend was travelling along the ridge and decided to try the scenic route."

"How 'bout taking a dive and lookin' around?"

Jack blinked. Hale had mentioned that he, like Jack, was a certified scuba diver. But diving into a deep undersea ridge like Iozima with just a divesuit for protection against the pressure was not particularly realistic, and he said so.

"That's not the sort of diving I mean," Hale said with a smile. "The Institute has a titanium submersible."

For what seemed like the millionth time since meeting Hale, Jack felt a pang of envy. There were only a handful of such submersibles in the world. Jack fondly remembered seeing the demonstration of Graham Hawkes's submersible *Deep Flight* in Monterey, but he never dreamed he'd get the opportunity to ride in one. "You famous scientists get all the good toys."

"Stop complaining—it's not like they'd trust *me* with a tranq rifle."

"Good point," Jack said with a grin, then looked at his watch. "How soon can you get it over here?"

"Depends on who's usin' it right now," Hale said, bending over to rummage through the detritus from the dining room table, eventually liberating his cordless phone. "Worst case, we won't get it till morning." He pushed the phone's TALK button and then dialed a sequence of numbers. "Hello, Josie, it's Ralph...I'm doin' just fine, darlin'. Listen, who's got the *Scorpion Fish*?...All right, can you patch me through to him?...Beauty....Yes, I'll hold."

Hale put his hand over the mouthpiece and looked at Jack. "Grant Wilhoite's one of my bright boys. I got him studyin' geothermal—" He cut himself off, taking his hand off the mouthpiece. "Grant?...Grant, it's Ralph...Ralph *Hale*, your boss...That's right, mate. Listen, I need you to fetch the *Scorp* down to me on Malau...What do you...yes, I know, Grant, I'm the one who *gave* you that deadline, so I don't mind if you blow it. It's for a good cause. Now—what?...Look, mate, I know the project's important, but I've got a lizard here out of a Ray Harryhausen movie, three dead people, and one injured copper. That takes precedent, okay?...Glad you think so. So get your arse down here...Right, I'll see you first thing in the morning."

As Hale pushed the END button and put the cordless down on the table, Jack smiled. "*Scorpion Fish*, huh?"

"Trust me, when you see the thing, you'll know why."

"I don't doubt it." He leaned over the table, moving the satellite photos off the maps. "Okay, since we're going to *have* a submersible, we should figure out where we're going to take it."

Later on, Jack left Hale to his afternoon nap and went to pick Brandon up from the *Malau Weekly News* offices.

"He didn't ask too many annoying questions, did he?" Jack asked the reporter with a grin.

"Nah, I'd say I won the Annoying Questions Derby," Paul replied.

Brandon nodded emphatically. "Big time. But I know how to use Quark now."

Jack frowned. "I assume that isn't a subatomic particle?"

Paul laughed. "A computer program. It's what I use to lay out the paper. So where you guys off to?"

"Feeding time at the zoo," Jack said. "Our overgrown newt out there should be awake enough to feel peckish."

"Sounds like fun. Oh, hey, listen—"

"Yeah?" Jack said.

"Don't let Derek get to you. I mean, he's a complete and total asshole, no question. We've sorta gotten used to him. He keeps catching good fish, and we let him be a total asshole, and generally completely ignore him." Paul scratched his cheek. "I guess what I'm saying is, he isn't worth getting worked up over. No one around here takes him seriously—no reason why you should."

Jack smiled ruefully. He *had* let Derek get to him, to a manner Jack wouldn't have believed possible. "Thanks. C'mon, humble assistant, let's go do some work."

Brandon grinned. "Okay, Dad."

As they walked toward the beach, Brandon asked, "So what'd you and Doc Hale do all day?"

Jack gave his son a précis of what he and Hale learned. "So we'll be going out in the submersible tomorrow morning when Hale's man gets it here." He hesitated. *How do I tell him? Oh, hell, just come out and say it.* Speaking the words quickly, he said, "It'll just be the two of us. I really wish I could take you along, but it's just too dangerous. I can't put you at risk like that—"

"That's okay," Brandon said with a shrug. "I understand."

"You do?" Jack was stunned. *An alien came down and replaced my son with a pod person.* Brandon *hated* being left out of things. "You're not upset?"

"Nah, I got plenty of stuff to do around here."

Jack marvelled at the resiliency of the preadolescent boy. Two days ago, Brandon was throwing a hissy fit because Jack wouldn't take him out in Hale's seaplane, requiring bribery and paternal convincing. Now, Jack wasn't entirely sure he'd have been able to talk Brandon into *coming* on the *Scorpion Fish*.

Kids, he thought, *go figure.*

"Got enough time in your busy schedule to help me feed Superlizard?"

"Oh, sure," Brandon said agreeably.

"Good. Salamanders are big on invertebrates, so I figure we can start with that. Having sampled the local mud crabs, I can't imagine that our boy won't go for them."

"Maybe," Brandon said.

Within a half-hour, they had gathered a bucketful of mollusks and mud crabs. Brandon had seemed less than enthusiastic about the choice of food, which Jack thought odd.

"What if he doesn't like this stuff?" he asked.

Jack smiled. "Oh, I think he will."

"Yeah, but what if he doesn't?"

He should know this as well as I do, Jack thought, confused. *Hell, sometimes I think he knows it better. If you don't know the species of what you're feeding, try the food of the animal's closest analogue. Well, the thing only has a miniscule resemblance to a salamander, but that's a miniscule more than it resembles anything else outside of* Jurassic Park. *So we start with aquatic salamander food.*

Aloud, he said, "I'll switch from an aquatic diet to a terrestrial one. You know, bugs, leaves, that kind of thing."

"And if he doesn't like that?"

"We start from scratch."

Brandon nodded, then continued gathering invertebrates in silence. After a moment, Jack said, "Brandon—

the past year, all the running around we've done...has it been okay for you?"

Shrugging, Brandon said, "Yeah."

"I mean, it's been—fun, hasn't it?" Jack struggled with the words.

Another shrug. "Sure."

Dammit, Brandon, I'm not looking for polite answers here. "I mean, it's a lot better than sitting around and feeling sorry for ourselves, right?"

Yet another shrug. "Right." Brandon held up his bucket. "I'm full up."

Jack sighed. Obviously, Brandon didn't want to talk about whatever it was that seemed to be bothering him. *Maybe I'm imagining it.*

They went to the pier and dropped the various fish over the top of the cage. It fell into the water with a *plop!*

And then it stayed there. Superlizard recoiled from the food, then simply stared at it.

Dammit.

"See?" Brandon said, sounding entirely too self-satisfied. "He doesn't like it."

Jack looked more closely at the beast. He stared at Jack and Brandon as much—no, more than he did at the food. "I think we're making him uptight. Let's leave him alone. He'll eat, I'm sure of it," he said, more for Brandon's benefit, since in fact he wasn't at all sure.

I'll come back in an hour with some bugs and leaves, and take it from there, he decided.

"C'mon," he said, "let's get some dinner. Dr. Hale told me about a Japanese place on the other side of the island, and I could go for some tempura right about now."

"Yeah, okay." Brandon seemed less than enthused, even though he loved Japanese food. *What is with him?* he wondered.

Diane would know what was wrong, he thought, then quashed it. This was no time to get maudlin.

We'll have a nice dinner, then try to feed the big lizard. Tomorrow, Hale and I will explore, and maybe get to the bottom of this little mystery.

He focused on that. It was easier than trying to figure out his son.

SIX

Malau Police Chief Joseph Movita hated hospitals. If you were in a hospital, it meant something had gone wrong, that somebody had screwed up. One of the reasons Joe became a police officer was so that he would be in a position to keep things from going wrong and people from screwing up. So a visit to Doctor Hart's clinic was not something he especially wanted to do, since it made it feel like he hadn't done his job.

But he hadn't much of a choice. Jimmy was convalescing here, and he wouldn't be much of a boss if he didn't visit a subordinate who'd been injured in the line of duty.

Joe had been born on the very day that the United States Marine Corps liberated the island—which, if nothing else, made it very easy for people to remember his birthday. His mother had been with a group of Malauans who had hidden in the jungle—his father had been killed six months previously by Japanese soldiers after he protested the living conditions on Malau since the war started. A Marine named Joseph Toriccelli had found Tara Movita and the others in the jungle and stayed with them in case any Japanese soldiers happened upon them to try to get in one final shot before the USMC nailed them. In the middle of this, his mother went into labor. Private Toriccelli knew almost nothing about how to deliver a baby beyond a half-remembered training film, but somehow he managed to do it in the middle of a humid jungle. In his honor, the boy was named Joseph Toriccelli Movita, and the private made his godfather.

Chief Movita had only met the man who delivered him once, but he didn't remember it. He was only three at the time, and the newly promoted Sergeant Toriccelli had made good on a promise to visit his godson on the island he helped liberate. Shortly afterward, he was assigned to the fighting in Korea, and was killed.

A father killed for trying to make people's lives easier; a godfather who was a soldier killed in the line of duty. No wonder he became Malau's "top cop."

Jimmy lay on one of the clinic's flat, uncomfortable-looking beds, reading a motorcycle magazine. Bandages covered several parts of his chest and arms and an IV drip lead to a vein in his arm.

"How's it going, Jimmy?"

The young cop looked up and smiled at Joe. "Not too bad, Chief. It only hurts when I breathe." He set the magazine aside. Joe saw that he was reading about a new Suzuki model, and remembered that Jimmy had been saving up to buy a Suzuki.

The chief smiled. "Well, the doc says you should be all right in a couple of weeks."

"So," Jimmy said after a moment, "what'd you do with the body?"

Joe's smile fell into a frown. "Body?"

"Y'know, T. rex out there. Did you chop it up into cutlets for Manny or what? Hope you didn't try blowing it up. There were these people in the States that tried that, and they got whale guts all over—" Jimmy cut himself off, looking at Joe.

The chief closed his eyes for a moment. Obviously Jimmy read Joe's expression.

Before Joe could say anything, Jimmy said, "That goddamn thing's still alive, isn't it?"

"For the time being, yeah."

"But—"

"The order came straight from Manny," Joe said before Jimmy could say any more. "Look, we don't know what the thing is, and we have to—"

"We know *exactly* what it is, Chief!" Jimmy said, shouting now. "It's a killer! It got those two women and Dak, and it would've killed me!"

Probably at the sound of her patient shouting, Doctor Hart came dashing into the room. "What's going on?"

Jimmy was trying to sit up now. "Chief, you gotta kill that thing!"

The doctor put her hands on Jimmy's shoulders, gently guiding him back into a prone position. "Take it easy," she said.

"It's caged up, Jimmy," Joe said. "It can't harm anyone right now."

"But what if there're more of 'em? Jesus, Chief, it—"

Doctor Hart spoke more forcefully this time: "I said take it easy, Jimmy."

Jimmy closed his eyes and took a breath. Then he opened them again and looked at Joe. "You gotta promise me, Chief—if that thing gets loose, you'll take it down."

Joe Movita thought about the father he never met. When the war started, the Japanese administrators—who had always been viewed as authoritarian but fair—were recalled and replaced with a military government, led by a unpleasant colonel named Takeshewada, who turned the island into a police state. When Kile Movita tried to object to the conditions, tried to buck the authority on the island, Colonel Takeshewada had him killed.

Joe wondered, if it came to that, if he could do the same in order to fulfill a promise to one of his people.

"I'll do what I can," was what he finally said.

Then he turned on his heel and walked out of the clinic.

As soon as Dad was out of sight of Manny's—having gone off to meet Doctor Hale at the pier for their little underwater trip—Brandon gulped down the rest of his orange juice, took a final bite of scrambled egg, and dashed out of the restaurant. (Dad had already covered the tab.)

On his way to the lagoon, he passed a candy store, and decided to splurge and get himself a bag of cheese puffs. He just had to remember to wash his hands when he was done, so Dad wouldn't notice the orange residue on his fingers. Dad hated it when Brandon had cheese puffs right after breakfast, but to the boy's mind it was one of the essentials in life.

After paying for the cheese puffs—only fifty cents for a bag that would've cost a dollar back home—he continued into the jungle, hoping that the jar of bugs and leaves and such were still there.

He hadn't been able to get away from Dad the previous day, except when he was with Paul. He couldn't really run off then, either, without raising suspicion—especially with all those weird looks Paul had been giving him. After dinner, Dad had taken Brandon back to the hotel and told him to stay there, just in case. Brandon had toyed with the idea of sneaking out to try to feed Casey, but then Dad had said he and Doctor Hale were going to investigate the jungle, see if they could figure out what it was the big guy wanted there.

Based on what Dad had said at breakfast that morning,

they hadn't found Casey—*thank God*, he thought, remembering both Chief Movita's words about protecting the island and Paul's comment about humanity and nature—which meant that it was more imperative that Brandon try to feed the little guy.

Besides, if I find out what he eats, I can help Dad feed the big one.

When he arrived back at the lagoon, he was grateful to find that the pile of branches and leaves he had hidden the sample jars under remained undisturbed. He pulled them out, then went to his usual spot on the shore of the lagoon. He upended the jar, and various bugs and leaves fell onto the ground in front of him.

Then he sat cross-legged in front of his second attempt at a lizard buffet, ripped open the bag of cheese puffs, and waited.

After about a minute, Casey popped his head up from the water. *Good, he hasn't gone anywhere.* But he also looked *real* bad. The dog for whom Brandon had named Casey always looked like that after going through the dog run for an hour. *He's all low on energy. Geez, hasn't he eaten anything?*

As Casey approached, Brandon set down the bag of cheese puffs, wiping his hands on his shorts.

"C'mon, little guy. *Please* eat."

Casey inspected the food, then once again rejected it, letting out a pitiful whine.

"Great. What am I gonna do? If I tell anybody about you, you could end up in a lab, or dead. Please, you *gotta* eat."

Casey looked down at the bag of cheese puffs. Brandon noticed that a few had spilled out onto the ground. He was about to pick them up and drop them in the sample jar to throw away later—

—when Casey went over and nibbled on a puff. Then he gobbled one down.

Then another. Then another.

"Wow," Brandon muttered. He dumped the bag's remaining contents onto the ground. Casey attacked the puffs with gusto. "Wherever you come from, they've got junk food. This is *amazing*."

He wondered how he was going to convince Dad to feed cheese puffs to Superlizard.

It had been a couple of years since Jack Ellway saw the demonstration of the submersible *Deep Flight*, but he didn't remember it at all resembling a scorpion fish. Such fish spent most of their time lying on reefs pretending to be rocks—indeed, they were sometimes referred to as rockfish or stonefish. One of his colleagues once joked that the preferred scientific term for them was "ugly buggers." *Deep Flight* had looked a lot more like a manta, so he was curious as to why Hale had chosen the name *Scorpion Fish* for his own submersible.

When he saw it bobbing in the water tethered to the pier opposite the nine-foot lizard, he understood. The submersible was the same proportional shape as a stonefish, the same basic color, and even had portholes where the eyes would have been. He could see the outlines of mechanical arms but, retracted as they were, they seemed to be part of the smooth surface.

What really worried him was the size. The thing looked barely big enough to hold one person, let alone three.

Hale, Paul, and a tall man approximately Jack's age were waiting for him at the pier. "Ready to go, Jack?" Hale said, all smiles.

"Guess so."

"Glad to hear it, mate. Oh, this is Grant Wilhoite. Grant, Jack Ellway."

Wilhoite simply grunted as he shook Jack's hand. He didn't look especially happy to be here. Based on the half of his conversation with Hale that Jack had heard the previous day, he suspected that Wilhoite had postponed a project near and dear to his heart in order to keep his boss happy. Jack knew how he'd feel in the man's place. *But then, there may well be lives at stake—not to mention finding a new species. I'd say it's worth it.*

"So," Paul said, "you guys headed to the Iozima Ridge?"

"That's the plan," Jack said.

"Well, don't forget to bring me back a souvenir," he said with a grin, as he brought his camera up to his eye. "Say cheese." He snapped one picture, then another.

Wilhoite tapped his foot impatiently. "Can we get a bleedin' move on?"

Hale grinned at Paul. "I think you'd better stick with candid shots from here on in, mate."

"Right," Paul said.

After the reporter took a few more pictures and said his goodbyes, Hale climbed into the *Scorpion Fish*, then Jack followed—Wilhoite came a moment later after untethering the submersible from the pier. Jack's fears about the *Scorp*'s capacity were, he realized quickly, justified. Hale had said the vessel was made of titanium, and the thing's skin was thick enough to make the inside even more cramped. The seats barely managed the width of the average human rear end and they had no leg room to speak of. Hale helped Jack harness himself in while Wilhoite strapped himself. Then Hale got himself secured while the pilot started things up.

"Whenever you're ready, Grant," Hale said, and within moments, the view outside the porthole next to Jack's seat changed from one of Malau's beaches to blue water.

The sea life he saw initally pretty much matched his expectations. First there were bits of kelp and plankton, plus the usual collection of mud crabs and mollusks. As they went deeper, and Wilhoite activated the *Scorp*'s external halogen lamps, he saw dozens of lionfish, their plumes of blue fins rippling in the water; tiger groupers; flounders; he even caught sight of a silvertip shark off in the distance. When they neared a reef, he saw a genuine scorpion fish, pretending to be a rock, as expected; the amber and brown beauty of a flatworm; the festive colors of nudibranchs crawling along; angel fish of all varieties. The rainbow of colors never ceased to amaze Jack— nothing on land could compare to the beauty of the world under the sea.

He recalled the first time he took Diane scuba diving. It was at UCSD, after they'd been dating for a month. She said she'd always loved sitting and staring at the ocean, and Jack just laughed. "Sitting and staring at the surface of the ocean," he said, "is like going to a museum and only looking at the picture frames." She was dubious, but she took the certification course and then went with Jack on a dive. Within a month of that first dive, she'd switched to a marine biology major. A year after that, they got married.

And thirteen years later, she died.

Hale brought him out of his suddenly melancholy reverie. "We're at Iozima now, Jack," he said, then turned to the pilot. "Just keep a steady course along the ridge."

Wilhoite acknowledged with an "okay" gesture.

"Doesn't talk much, does he?" Jack stage-whispered to Hale.

"He's just cheesed off 'cause I took him off his project. He'd been waiting months for access to the *Scorp*, so I can't say as I blame him."

Smiling, Jack turned back to the porthole. This deep, the only illumination came from the *Scorp*'s lamps, and the natural fluorescence of some of the fish. He saw an angler fish, its needle-sharp teeth in search of something to munch on, the red and orange shape of a dumbo octopus, and a mess of tomopterids.

His left leg started to cramp, and he shifted as much as

he could within the harness—only to discover that his right leg had fallen asleep. *Wonderful.*

Hale noticed his discomfort. "Comfy, Jack?"

"Yeah, now that my legs have gone to sleep." He turned back to the porthole and remembered both the mechanical arms and Superlizard's dietary problems. "Let's collect some water and soil samples. If our amphibian is from around here, it'll feed on the sea life we bring back."

"Sounds like a plan," Hale said as he pushed a few buttons, then grabbed a pair of levers. These presumably controlled the mechanical arms, confirmed by the fact that Jack could see the arms moving in tandem with Hale's manipulations of the levers.

The levers flanked a video monitor that Jack hadn't noticed before. It appeared to feed from a camera mounted to the *Scorp*'s top, and it gave a better view of the arms' movements as it gathered samples from both the soil of the ridge and of the surrounding sea life.

"I've got a pretty fair sample," Hale said after about five minutes' worth of gathering. "Let's move on, shall we? Arms are—" he maneuvered the levers into their original position "—in place. Let's be off."

Again, Wilhoite made the "okay" gesture, and the *Scorp* started to move.

Then, suddenly, the vessel was jostled and came to a stop. It felt just like a car hitting the brakes, and Jack was grateful for the harness that kept him in place. "What the hell?" he said.

The engines were still running, though. Wilhoite said, "We're going full speed—at a dead stop!"

Jack peered out the porthole, trying to see what had happened. Maybe they were caught in something, or maybe a large fish had come down to block their path.

Suddenly, the *Scorp* was turned upside down. Jack was even more grateful for the harness. The map, satellite photos, and a few other odds and ends Hale had brought along weren't so lucky, and they clattered from the floor to the ceiling—which now *was* the floor.

Just as suddenly, the vessel was flipped back rightside up, and the jostling stopped.

Letting out the breath he hadn't even realized he was holding, Jack looked around to make sure the others were okay.

Then the lights flickered and went out.

Sunlight did not penetrate this deep—the only illumination one got was either artificial or came from the phosphorescent aquatic life. The former had been disabled, and the latter didn't seem to be around at the moment.

The *Scorp* was now in a darkness so complete and total, Jack felt like he was being smothered by a thick blanket.

"Oh my God," he said, hoping he didn't sound as panicked as he was starting to feel. His heart pounded so hard he was sure his ribs would crack.

"Hang on, Jack."

"Give it a moment."

He had no idea who spoke what phrase, or if either Hale or Wilhoite said both.

Then the interior lights flickered back on. They were only a bit dimmer than they had been before. *Thank God.*

Wilhoite said, "We've got maybe ten minutes of air left. We need to surface."

"No argument from me," Jack muttered.

"Go," Hale said.

Jack peered out the window, but the outside was as black as it was before the power was restored. "Damn— I can't see anything."

"We stirred up a lot of silt," Hale pointed out. " 'Sides, the external lamps are out as long as we're on emergency power."

"All right," Wilhoite said, "as you yanks say, we are outta here."

Jack fell back in his seat as the *Scorp* accelerated upward at a much faster rater than it had going on the way down. But then, with only ten minutes of air left, they couldn't afford to dillydally.

So what the hell was that that tossed us around like that?

He had his suspicions, and he didn't like them, not one bit.

Paul Bateman saw Ralph Hale's jeep approaching just as he was walking over to Manny's for lunch. He hadn't expected to see Hale and Jack so soon—Hale had said that he expected the trip to last well past lunch. Curious, he approached them as they parked it near Hale's bungalow.

Jack hauled a sealed container out of the jeep. Paul arrived right in the middle of a friendly, if heated, discussion.

"—don't know what the hell was happening out there, but we got batted around like a Ping-Pong ball. Whatever it was, it didn't like us."

"Jack, take it easy," Hale said. "It wasn't a creature. A creature that size couldn't spin a submersible around like a top. No, those quakes cause a lot of underwater turbulence."

"What happened?" Paul asked.

"The *Scorp* got knocked for a loop," Jack said. "Conked the power for a minute, then twirled us around like a dervish. I think it was one of Superlizard's relatives."

"And I still say it was another quake," Hale insisted.

Paul said, "We did get nailed with a pretty nasty quake while you were gone. One of my reference books fell over onto Mak's head while he was bringing the mail."

"See?" Hale said.

"I don't know."

Paul shook his head as the three of them started walking toward Hale's bungalow. *Figures. The marine biologist says it's aquatic life, the geologist says it was an earthquake.*

Aloud, he said, "Well, whatever it was, I've got an interesting tidbit for you guys. I checked the Internet for facts about the Iozima Ridge. In the 1960s, when a lot of pesticides were banned, an international group of chemical companies dumped thousands of concrete containers into the Pacific—over the Iozima Ridge. Concrete *can* leak, you know."

Jack stopped walking. Paul turned to face him; Hale did likewise. Jack had an expression that made Paul want to look for the light bulb on top of his head.

"What're you thinkin', Jack?" Hale asked.

"I'm thinking about frogs."

Paul raised an eyebrow. "This a common thing with marine biologists, or is it just you?"

"No, I'm serious," Jack said. "You've got Internet access, right?" he asked Hale.

"Yeah, 'course."

"Good. I want to show you a particular web site."

"Why don't we do this in my office?" Paul said.

Hale asked, "What difference does it make?"

"I know for a fact that you just have a 28.8 modem and your ISP's in Melbourne, so the phone charge is probably an arm and a leg. I, on the other hand, have a T1 line and free access."

Hale's eyes widened. "How the hell'd you manage that one?"

Paul grinned. "Friends in low places. C'mon."

Still carrying the container—Jack said it contained fish and soil samples from Iozima—they walked at a

brisk pace to Paul's office. Paul sat at his computer—
which he never turned off—and tapped the mouse button,
clearing the screensaver of a nude centerfold, then
clicked over to his web browser. Jack rolled his eyes at
the screensaver; Hale just grinned. The pair of them
flanked Paul as he said, "Okay, shoot."

Jack gave him the URL, which Paul dutifully typed in.
Within seconds, he was looking at pictures of mutated
frogs.

"Yuck," was Paul's first comment.

"Mutated frogs," Jack said, "with extra eyes and extra
limbs. Discovered in contaminated ponds—first in
Minnesota, then in Vermont, California, Québec…"

Hale rubbed his chin. "So our poor big friend could be
some kind of mutation?"

Jack shrugged. "Frogs and salamanders are part of the
same biological order. Which means they could have
similar biochemical reactions to ingesting pesticides."

"I can do a preliminary analysis," Hale said, looking
down at the container. "Enough to detect chemical traces,
anyhow."

Jack blinked. "You have that kind of equipment?"

"Mostly. Between my gear, and the stuff Alyson's got
in her lab at the clinic, I should be able to do it."

"Okay. Hey, Paul, where's Brandon? He'd enjoy being
part of this."

Paul shrugged. "I haven't seen him. Been cooped up
here all day."

"All right—I want to take a shot at feeding the beast
with what we collected. Once the good doctor takes his
sample, you wanna give me a hand with the feeding?"

"Sure," Paul said with a smile. *What the heck*, he
thought, *it's a photo op.*

Within half an hour, Paul and Jack had rigged a metal

trough full of what Jack said was a representative sample of the general vicinity of Iozima to a pulley. "In theory," Jack said, "it should treat this stuff like a home-cooked meal." He sighed. "Certainly, it hasn't liked anything else we've thrown at it."

Placing the pulley by the shark cage, the two of them carefully lowered the trough into the cage. The big lizard remained submerged up to its neck, leaving plenty of room for the trough to swing on the pulley as they lowered it.

Once the trough was about halfway down the above-water part of the cage, Jack said, "Okay, let's hold it there." They secured the rope.

The creature then rose up out of the water slowly. Paul swore the thing looked like a vulture as it arced up and over the trough. It smelled the contents for a moment, then shoved its snout in. Within seconds, it was hungrily devouring the contents.

"It recognizes the taste," Jack said. He pumped his fist and said, "Yes! Finally!"

"Nice work," Paul said.

"Well, the Iozima Ridge is its home."

Hale approached just then. "Found the right diet, yeah?"

"So it would seem," Jack said proudly.

"Well, I've got news. It looks like your suspicion was right, Jack. I found traces of DDT in the water sample."

Paul frowned. "Meaning?"

"DDT accumulates in the fatty tissues of organisms," Jack said, "and becomes more concentrated as it works its way up the food chain."

Paul rolled his eyes. "Meaning?" he repeated, more forcefully.

"It means that this creature is not a biological anomaly. It was mutated by a concentrated diet of artificial chemicals."

Jesus Christ, what is it about scientists that they can't speak English? For a third time, Paul said, "Meaning?"

"Meaning, we created a monster," Jack said. "and it's probably not the only one of its kind."

Paul decided he liked the scientific gobbledygook better.

SEVEN

Pierce Askegren reached up as high as his right arm would go and pressed the button on his Nikon just as the five men entered the hotel lobby and went out of sight. He sighed, hoping that he actually got one of the band members in the shot and not just a piece of ground or the wall of the hotel's second floor or something.

Pierce made his living as a freelance photographer, specializing in candid photographs of celebrities. Unfortunately, thousands of others made their living the same way. If you weren't lucky enough to be at the front of the throng when a particular group of celebrities made their appearance, you had to count on unreliable shots like the one he just took.

He lit a cigarette, then stared at the light flickering from his Zippo. For a minute, he imagined Marissa Michaels, his editor, standing on the flame, her feet burning in agony. *Damn her anyway*, he thought with a snarl as he blew smoke into the South Seas air. *Okay, so*

George Clooney got that restraining order against the paper. Is that my fault?

According to Marissa, it was, and as punishment, he got saddled with following around the hot new rock band, a group with the semi-ironic name of the Don't Quit Your Day Job Players, on a world tour promoting their album *TKB*. As far as Pierce was concerned, they were just a bunch of white guys with long hair—except for the drummer, who was a white guy with a buzz cut.

Ah, well, he thought, *it could've been worse. She could've given me the Spice Girls.*

Pierce took another drag on his cigarette, then wiped the sweat from his bald pate. A Washington, D.C. native, he hated the humidity of this insipid little tourist trap of an island. But the Don't Quit Your Day Job Players had a stop in Kalor—to be followed by dates in Manila and Tokyo—and so he was stuck here until they left.

A voice with a thick Italian accent said from behind him, *"Ah, bello!"*

Sighing, Pierce turned around to see Marcello Silverio. Pierce first met the *paparazzo* when they both had the David Hasselhoff beat three years earlier. They re-encountered each other on the plane to Kalor—apparently the DQYDJPs were huge in Italy.

"Hi, Mark," Pierce said with a dearth of enthusiasm.

Marcello winced. He hated being called Mark, which is why Pierce kept it up. "I got a lovely shot of the band. *Perfecto.*"

Pierce sighed. *Days like this, I think I should've listened to Ma and become a plumber.*

"Lads!" came another voice, this one belonging to John Hawkins. Pierce had known and respected Hawk for years. The man always managed to get the most amazing shots. He also had a handsome face and was eloquent as hell. As a result, he was perfect for playing the public face of celebrity photographers whenever there was a backlash of some sort against the practice. After Princess Diana's death, Hawk had gone onto some BBC news program or other and carried on for half an hour about the dignity of the press and the necessity for freedom of expression, and various other bits of bullshit. The next day, he was hiding in Fergie's bushes, trying to get a shot of her sunbathing.

"I just overheard a couple of tourists who've been on Malau," Hawk was saying. "Some kind of creature was captured over there."

Hawk may have been a master, but he tended to let his imagination run away with him. For years, he had insisted that he had genuine Loch Ness Monster pictures—"Not fakes like those other johnnies, this was the goods, pictures of the whole bleedin' Loch Ness Monster family!"—so Pierce couldn't help but say, "Yeah, right. Elvis's alien baby."

"No, this is legit. They both saw it. A nine-foot lizard that can walk on its hind legs."

Pierce scratched his ample belly. "How much you have to pay for this 'legit' sighting?" he asked, sarcasm still lacing his tone.

Hawk looked indignant. "Please. I am a member of the free press. I have standards. I overheard it like any proper journalist."

Lightning arced in the twilight sky, followed moments later by a thunderclap.

Pierce sighed. "All right, fine, a couple guys in Hawaiian shirts with disposable cameras in their khaki shorts pockets think they see a big lizard—"

"Actually, they were dressed in T-shirts and denim shorts, and one of them wore a Harvard ring. Class of '88."

Marcello frowned. "How close *were* you?"

Hawk shrugged. "Good ears and a telephoto lens. Look, do you want to sit around waiting for a bunch of rock stars to resurface from their drunken orgies long enough to pose for a bad picture, or do you want a scoop?"

Pierce had to admit to himself that Hawk had a point. But, as another bolt of lightning struck, a thought occurred. "Since when does John Hawkins offer to split a scoop?"

"Ah yes, well, you see, in order to find the thing, we'll need to rent a boat."

"Find it? You said it was captured."

Hawk rolled his eyes. "You're being too bloody linear, me old mucker. Remember my Loch Ness photos? Where there's smoke, there's fire, and where there's one big lizard—"

Marcello smiled. "There's got to be a *famiglia*. *Excellente!* So where is the boat?"

"Ah, yes, well, that is the problem, my dear old friends and colleagues, you see—I'm a bit strapped for cash at the moment, and—"

"Strapped?" Pierce said, incensed. Hawk always wore the most expensive clothes, had top of the line camera equipment, and threw money around like he had it to burn.

Marcello asked, "What happened to *Signor* 'Hello Ladies, I Have a Full Expense Account, Come Have Sex with Me,' *hanh*?"

Hawk at least had the good grace to look abashed. "Well, er, you see, I'm afraid that my full expense account is all, as it were—filled up. Cutbacks, you know."

"If we split the boat three ways down the middle," Marcello said, "I will go along."

"Fair enough," Hawk said.

"Look," Pierce said, not bothering to point out that a three-way split by definition couldn't be down the middle, "there's no way in hell I'm paying money to go out in the rain and look for a hypothetical monster. It just ain't gonna happen."

"Oh, come now, Pierce, that lightning doesn't mean anything. And we can rent a motorboat for next to nothing. Come now, what do you say?"

"I say forget it. No way."

Two hours later, Pierce sat in a motorboat for which he'd paid a third of the rental cost. The rain was coming down in buckets. *How the hell do I let myself get talked into these things?*

"Quite invigorating, isn't it?" Hawk said with the kind of grin that you just want to punch. "Why, all we need is a dog, and we'd have a Jerome K. Jerome book."

Pierce blinked. "What the hell're you talking about?"

"Oh, yes, I forgot, they don't read in your country, do they, Pierce?"

Snarling, Pierce said, "Yeah, well, we ain't got rulers who're inbred mutants, either."

"Nor do we, old chum. The royal family are simply a distraction to keep the general public from realize that the country is run by incompetents."

Shaking his head, Pierce said, "This is nuts. We should turn back."

"*Niente*," said Marcello, "I have sailed in worse."

"Of course *you* have," Pierce said, "you're insane." Marcello got his start by hanging upside down from the roof of a very famous—and very reclusive—Italian actress and getting pictures of her changing clothes, then walking into a local newspaper with the photos. Said roof was two hundred feet off the ground, as the actress lived in a villa in the Tuscan hills.

Marcello let loose with a string of Italian curses, which Pierce couldn't understand a word of, and so wasn't insulted by.

"Lighten up, lads. We're about to be famous."

Yeah, right, sure, Pierce thought. *What the hell am I*

doing here? This is nuts. This is absolutely, positively, cuckoo-bird–style nuts. I should—

He cut his thought off when he heard a sound in the water.

"What was that?" Marcello asked, relieving Pierce, as that meant that someone else heard it, too.

Pierce leaned forward, trying to filter out the sound of the rain coming down on the motorboat's canopy and the *rrrrrrr* noise of the motor.

Suddenly, for the first time, it hit him. *We're out here looking for the relatives of a nine-foot lizard. This is nuts. This is dangerous.*

"A porpoise, maybe?" Hawk ventured.

"Can we just get the hell out of here?" Pierce said, suddenly nostalgic for the humidity of Kalor and the monotony of chasing rock stars around the world.

Marcello shushed him and cut the motor.

Great. Now we're sitting ducks.

Pierce heard the sound again.

Then something bumped the boat.

Oh hell...

Marcello tried to start the motor, but it just coughed and died. Pierce pushed him out of the way. "Move it, Mark, you couldn't flush a toilet if instructions were written on the handle."

Pierce tried desperately to get the motor to turn over, but the thing just sputtered and died. *The points are probably all wet. Why the hell did that jackass turn the motor off?*

Before he could try again, he heard the noise again, this time accompanied by the boat rocking severely. Out of the corner of his eye, he saw movement. He whirled around to see a massive, green, scaly head break through the water. The head looked to be at least seven feet from neck to top, with tiny, beady eyes, a huge snout, and what looked like razor-sharp teeth.

Pierce had never seen anything like it in real life. It looked like some kind of weird dinosaur.

Faced with a creature whose head was as big as the boat he sat in, a monster with teeth the size of Missouri, a big lizard that could probably eat Pierce alive without even having to chew—Pierce did the only thing he could do.

He took its picture.

Next to him, Hawk and Marcello did the same.

Damn, Hawk was right, Pierce thought, all thoughts of recalcitrant motors and certain death banished from his mind, replaced with the image of showing these pictures to Marissa and seeing the look of abject gratitude on her face as she begged to pay him three times his usual fee. *We are going to be* famous*!*

Two huge arms broke through the surface only a few feet from the boat, causing it to rock even more. The arms moved up to shield the creature's eyes from the three flashes that probably seemed like a strobe light.

Then it dove back underwater.

This might not have been much of a problem—beyond the fact that it meant no more pictures—but for one feature of the creature's anatomy. Pierce had been wondering what the rest of the thing looked like, how many legs it had, that sort of thing.

He and the others found out the hard way that it had a tail, for when it dove back underwater, the tail flipped up above the surface, impeded only by the small motorboat.

Pierce didn't get a good enough look at the tail to see how large it was, but it certainly was big enough that the motorboat wasn't much of an impediment.

As Pierce went flying through the air and crashing into the Pacific Ocean, his first thought was, *Damn, the salt water'll ruin the film!*

His last thought before blacking out was, *Sorry, Ma, I should've been a plumber.*

EIGHT

The sun shone brightly through a cloudless sky, the fish obediently swam into the nets to be caught, and the humidity had fallen as low as one could expect for midsummer on a tropical island. It was the sort of day that inspired poets to write lines like, "God's in his heaven, all's right with the world."

Derek Lawson barely noticed it.

He thought about a nine-foot-long lizard. He thought about an arsehead of an American scientist and his arsehead son, and an Australian gob with too much time on his hands, and an American journalist with what the yanks called an attitude problem.

He thought about Fiji, and his ex-wife, and his clapped-out trawler.

He thought about a nine-foot-long lizard and how it could make a lot of the other things he thought about go away. And he thought about the phone call he'd made that morning.

"Hey, Derek, you alive in there?"

Naru's voice brought Derek back to earth. "Sorry, just thinkin'. And dreamin'"

"Well, *now* I'm scared."

"Ha ha ha. Look, I had big dreams when I was your age, mates. Very big dreams. Funny how a little back alimony and some unpaid income taxes can stuff up the best-laid plans, but—"

Kikko rolled his eyes. "Not the 'best-laid plans' speech *again*."

Naru laughed and covered his ears. "Not again, not again!"

Normally, Derek wouldn't mind the japing, but today he was in an especially foul mood. "My life's a joke, is it?"

"C'mon Derek," Kikko said, "enough of this. You got a great life. You live in the tropics, you own your own boat—"

"A boat that's almost ready to be scuttled," he said, just as the wheel pulled to the left, as it often did when he let his attention drift.

Naru picked up the ball. "We make nice money from the tourists, we're saving up for Fiji—"

"It's a pipe dream, mates," Derek interrupted. He was sick of pining for something he couldn't have. "Let's be honest, hey? Our little restaurant on the beach, lying in the sun all day, drinkin' beer with the tourists at night, settlin' down with sweet little native nymphs—we'll never have the money for it. Not in this lifetime." Derek sighed. *Bloody wonderful, now I'm depressing myself.*

He thought about a nine-foot lizard.

The hell with Ellway. That sucker's mine, and nothing's gonna stop me from makin' my mark with that monster.

"But what the hell," he said with a smile, "right?"

"Right, boss," Kikko said, slapping him on the back. "Besides, I may have a line on something that'll give

us a little something extra in the cash department.
Remember that Indonesian bloke we took deep-sea fishing? The one who was in the market for exotic species?"
Kikko and Naru both nodded. "Well, I rang him up. Told
him about our nine-footer. He's interested." Derek smiled.
"*Very* interested. If he likes what he sees, he'll buy it from
us for a bloody fortune."

Kikko and Naru exchanged glances. Naru said, "But it
isn't ours to sell."

Derek rolled his eyes. "Now you're sounding like that
American bastard. It's ours as much as anybody's. All
we've gotta do is haul it over to Kalor."

Again, Kikko and Naru looked at each other. Then
Kikko asked, "How much is 'a bloody fortune'?"

Derek smiled, but before he could answer, something
hit the boat with a light *thump*.

Derek looked around, but saw nothing untoward. *So
what the hell was that?*

Another *thump*.

This time he traced the noise to the port side. He ran
over to the railing, Kikko and Naru on his heels.

Peering over the side, he saw a small motorboat, capsized, bumping up against the trawler. As he was about to
make a disparaging comment about tourists leaving their
crap lying about, he noticed a person clutching onto the
side of the boat: a balding white bloke, wearing some
kind of rain slicker, and with a camera around his neck.

"C'mon," Derek said, "let's haul him up out of there."

Jack had come to the clinic searching for Brandon, only
to find the place abuzz with activity. Down the street,
Derek and his two hangers-on were heading toward the
police station with Chief Movita. *Great, what did that
idiot do this time?*

As he stepped up onto the verandah, Alyson came out.

"Hi," she said, momentarily startled by his presence.

"Hi yourself. I came looking for Brandon, but, uh—Well, what's going on?"

"Derek found some guy clutching to a capsized motorboat that washed up against his trawler. He was pretty badly injured, so he brought him here."

Jack tried and failed to feel guilty about his disappointment that Derek hadn't actually done anything wrong.

Alyson continued, "His wallet identifies him as Pierce Askegren. He's got a batch of press credentials, and he had a fairly sophisticated camera around his neck."

"How badly is he hurt?"

"Not too awful—a few bumps and bruises, and some nasty scratches. Familiar-looking scratches."

Jack saw where this was going. "Same as on Jimmy and Dak?"

"Not quite the same—bigger. A lot bigger. Plus, he's been mumbling about a monster."

"He must've gotten wind of our amphibian." Jack scratched his chin. "If Paul can salvage any of the film from his camera, we might get a clue what he was up to."

Alyson nodded. "That's a good idea. I'll get the camera."

Within minutes, after Alyson had retrieved the camera and left instructions for the nurse, they went to the *Malau Weekly News* office. Paul had just come out of the darkroom when they arrived, so he took the camera and went back in.

After what seemed to Jack like an appallingly long time, he came back out. "I'll have prints in about five minutes," Paul said.

"You could salvage it?" Jack asked. Given how much salt water the camera had taken in, he and Paul had both been half-convinced that the film would be ruined.

"Luck of the stupid. Only five exposures had been made, then the guy must've hit the rewind button at some point. The camera's wrecked, but the film was all rolled up, so it was spared the worst of it. Back in a minute."

He went back in, then came out a few minutes later with an eight-by-ten print.

Jack looked down at what the image showed. *Holy shit.*

"I don't believe it," Alyson muttered. "Though it would explain the claw marks."

Tearing his gaze away from the photo, Jack looked at the reporter. "Paul, call President Moki and the chief. We need to talk about this, and *now.*"

Ten minutes later, the president closed his restaurant to all but Jack, Alyson, Paul, Chief Movita, Dr. Hale, and himself. They all stood around one of the larger tables, Moki holding Paul's print in hand.

All of them kept staring at it. The creature it portrayed was a dead ringer for Superlizard, except it didn't have the various horns. It also showed two other men taking pictures, and based on the scale, the lizard had to be at least thirty-five feet tall, maybe more. *It looks like Superlizard has a Mom*, Jack thought.

"Surely, this cannot be real," Moki said.

"It's not a double exposure," Paul said, pointing to the two photographers in the foreground, "the images would-n't be this solid. And the film was still in the camera."

"So all of you believe we have a creature of this size somewhere in our waters," Moki said.

And you don't? Jack almost blurted out, but managed to restrain himself. Instead, he pointed out the one fact that was obvious to his trained eye. "And who's it the spitting image of? Our nine-foot captive. Except for the horns, of course, but that means it's probably female. I think Mom is coming to bust her kid out of jail."

That left the room silent for several seconds. Then, finally, Paul said, "We've gotta let people know."

Jack almost smiled. *Typical journalist.*

"There'd be mass panic," Alyson pointed out.

"Not as much as there would be if this thing showed up *unannounced,*" Paul said, and Jack had to admit that his logic was spot-on.

The chief was shaking his head with something like awe. "I have seven officers—six, with Jimmy laid up. I am not equipped to deal with mass panic *or* a giant creature."

Moki, too, shook his head. "No, this is beyond us now. I will call Colonel Wayne at Fort MacArthur on Kalor."

Jack fought down a panic attack. *The last thing we need now is some military nutcase blowing everything up.* "Wait, wait—calling out the troops—" He cut himself off, choosing his words carefully. He *was* still an outsider here, but the president had trusted his judgment up to a point. *With any luck, I won't go past that point now.* "A thing like that can take on a life of its own. We need to decide what we want the military to do. What's this Colonel Wayne guy like?"

"Quite reasonable for a man in his position," Moki said without hesitation. Jack knew enough about Malau's president to know that, while he was diplomatic, he was not a liar. That he gave that answer, and so readily, meant that this colonel *should* be okay.

Jack had to hope that he had read Manny Moki correctly. "Let's talk to him alone, first."

Paul said, "By chopper, he could be here in no time."

"Then let's get him over here right away," Jack said, "without telling him why."

Moki nodded. "That is very prudent." He smiled. "Are you sure you are not a politician, Jack?"

Jack chuckled in reply as the president went over to the phone. *Geez, a mother lizard,* he thought. *Brandon's gonna—*

Oh, Christ. Brandon.

Aloud, he said, "I need to find Brandon."

"I'll do it," Alyson said.

"Thanks," Jack said, relieved. He didn't want to miss

the colonel's arrival, but he didn't want to go all day without even seeing his son.

Colonel J. Christopher Wayne really hated the tropics.

He never told anyone this, of course. After all, he'd been assigned to head up the United States Marine Corps base on Kalor Island, and Colonel Wayne did what he was told. It's like his drill sergeant used to tell him: *When you wear a green tuxedo, you dance where they tell you.*

Wayne missed very little about the ghettos of Philadelphia, but one of those was the winter weather. Tons of snow, huge drifts, snowmen built up in the playgrounds, icicles dripping from the fire escapes—that was winter. Right now, back home, gusts were blowing at thirty miles an hour back in Philly, with temperatures in the twenties.

As he wiped the sweat from his brow, Wayne almost wished he was there.

Almost. Born John Christopher LaMarre, his mother married Robert Wayne when John was six. Not wanting to be saddled with being named after a white Western star, John started going by his middle name after that. With the marriage came an older brother, whom the newly christened Christopher Wayne thought was God's gift. Greg was thirteen, knew all the cool guys in the neighborhood, and always made sure that Christopher was safe. When Mattie Phillips started beating Christopher and his best friend Andy up for their allowances, Greg said he'd take care of it. Mattie never bothered Christopher or Andy again.

Christopher knew nothing of gangs and guns and intimidation until after they found Greg's body in an alley. He heard those words from the immensely tall homicide detective who kept coming back to the house for a full two weeks after Greg died.

Only then did Christopher's nine-year-old mind realize exactly why Mattie stopped bothering him.

After that, he started really paying attention to his surroundings. He noticed that the "cool guys" in the neighborhood were the ones who usually didn't live to the age of twenty. He understood that nobody outside the ghetto gave a damn about the people inside it, so nobody inside gave a damn, either.

He decided to get out. The best way, to his mind, was the Armed Forces. When he was old enough, he didn't wait to be drafted for the Vietnam War, he enlisted with the Marines. The Corps provided him with something the ghetto never had: discipline. Things were ordered in the Marines; you followed a chain of command, you followed a procedure. Christopher Wayne thrived in that environment. He was a colonel by the age of forty-five, decorated many times, as a corporal in Vietnam and as a colonel in the Gulf War.

Any situation that came up, Wayne knew how to deal with it. The Corps had a procedure for pretty much anything you cared to name.

Wayne believed that, right up until he arrived on Malau—which was, if anything, even more oppressively humid than Kalor—and was introduced to Jack Ellway and a caged, nine-foot-long lizard.

After Ellway gave the full story of what had happened on Malau over the past few days, he muttered, "Good God." He couldn't believe it. If Manny Moki, Joe Movita, Paul Bateman, and Ralph Hale hadn't been with Ellway, he *wouldn't* have believed it. But he knew all four men—besides which, he could not deny the evidence of his own eyes. There in the cage sat a creature that looked like it came out of one of those monster movies he and Andy used to sneak into when they were kids.

He looked down at the photograph that Ellway had given him, apparently taken by some idiot *paparazzo*. *As if this one wasn't bad enough*, he thought, *its Mama's out there somewhere. An AWAC might be able to track it from the air. I could contact the 31ˢᵗ MEU on Okinawa...*

"That's the scale of operation we're trying to avoid here, Colonel," Ellway said, taking Wayne aback. The colonel hadn't realized he was speaking out loud. *Bad discipline, soldier*, he admonished himself.

Ellway continued: "Look, it's my belief that the giant creature is searching for its offspring. I say we give it what it wants."

Even Hale seemed surprised at that one. "Let the nine-footer go?" the geologist said.

"Why not capture the big one?" Wayne asked.

"How? And how do we know we could do it without killing it? It took almost a dozen tranq darts just to put Junior here down. And even if we got it, where do we keep it? I say we tag the nine-footer, then release it. We'll be able to tell if it's leading the giant creature away, and to where. Then we could come back and study them."

Wayne looked down at the picture of the Mama Lizard again. He remembered reading that they did that with whales and other large aquatic creatures in captivity—let them back into their natural environment, but put computerized tracking devices on them so they could be monitored.

Finally, it hit Wayne what the thing in the cage—and the one in the photo—reminded him of. Andy had had a pet gecko when he and Wayne were both ten. Andy loved that gecko, showed it more love than most kids showed to a dog or a cat. One day, he came home from school, and the thing was dead. They never did find out why, though Andy kept insisting that his stepfather killed it 'cause he never liked the thing. Both Andy and Wayne were devastated when Andy's mother flushed the gecko down the toilet.

"I'd like to keep these things alive," he finally said. "But I also have to protect my men and the people of Malau." He looked at Ellway. "How do we know the giant will see it?"

"We'll bring the captive to the open beach. I'll tag it, then everyone will clear the area and wait."

Not the most scientific approach—but then, how else would we do it? he thought. "All right," the colonel said, "but my people will be stationed and ready. I'll call it as I see it, is that understood?"

Ellway nodded. *Good*, Wayne thought. *The last thing we need now is some egghead nutcase screwing everything up.*

As they walked back to Wayne's helicopter, the colonel turned to Manny and Joe. "I'm gonna have to bring in two companies. Joe, I'm gonna need your help on this; keep your people off the beaches and out of the water—and out of my people's way."

"No problem," Joe said. "I've already got one officer laid up from that thing. I'm not in a rush for more."

"Neither am I. I'm willing to go along with this guy—" with his head, he indicated Ellway, walking several paces behind with Hale "—up to a point, but the minute that lives are in danger, I'm bringing the thing down."

They arrived at Wayne's chopper. To the pilot, he said, "Pat, radio the base."

"Yes, sir," Pat said. After a moment, the young sergeant handed Wayne the chopper radio.

"MacArthur, this is Wayne."

"Got you loud and clear, sir," came Corporal Macdonald's cheery voice.

"Get Alfa and Bravo mobilized and over to Malau ASAP. They're to report directly to me."

"Yes, *sir*. Anything else?"

"Keep everyone else on alert, just in case. Out."

A female voice cried out breathlessly, "I can't find Brandon. No one's seen him!"

Wayne turned to see that Doctor Alyson Hart had just run up to Ellway.

"He's lost? My God, by lunchtime, this place could be Guadalcanal."

Wayne snorted at the reference as Ellway came over to the others. "Brandon's missing. I gotta go look for him."

"I'll help you," Paul said.

Hale said, "I'll make sure the creature is on the beach and ready to be tagged."

Wayne turned to Joe. "Brandon?"

"Ellway's kid," the chief explained. "Twelve years old, going on thirty."

"Damn, we got a kid running around loose?" Wayne shook his head. "Better turn up soon. I do *not* want stragglers in case things get out of hand."

"Get no argument from me," Joe said.

Brandon was having the time of his life. He and Casey had spent hours together in the lagoon. Brandon had stocked up on cheese puffs that morning—the clerk made a comment about how his father wasn't going to like it when Brandon's teeth turned orange—and found Casey in his usual spot. Brandon was delighted to find that Casey liked eating the cheese puffs out of his hand in exactly the same way as his namesake did with the chopped-up bits of salami Mom always made for him.

After Casey finished one handful of puffs, and before Brandon could grab anymore, the little guy ran into the foliage.

Oh geez, what did I do now? Then he wondered if something else had come along to spook Casey, like his older brother tramping through the jungle being chased by humans had done before.

Then Casey peeked back out at Brandon. For a second, Brandon swore the little guy was smiling at him.

So Brandon smiled back. "Oh, you wanna play, huh?" he said as he ran toward Casey who, for his part, dashed back into the foliage.

For several minutes, they kept this little hide-and-seek game up, sweat dripping from Brandon's unkempt hair,

T-shirt coming untucked, shorts streaked with dirt, legs occasionally cramping from running around so much, and Brandon not caring about *any* of it, 'cause he and Casey were having fun. *I love this place.*

At first he didn't notice the python.

Only when Casey let out a tiny squeak—higher-pitched then the whine he used when Brandon had so much trouble feeding him—did Brandon see the huge snake suddenly show up in their path.

Brandon jumped back. He knew plenty about sea creatures, but next to nothing about snakes. He wasn't even entirely sure it was a python, and he had no idea whether or not a python was poisonous.

Casey obviously didn't know any more than he did— or he did know, and whatever it was was bad—because he ran off into the underbrush at top speed. Casey had been playful, only running at a speed that allowed the much slower Brandon to keep up. Now, though, the little guy was obviously scared out of his mind and was just running away.

Going in the same direction as the three-foot lizard, Brandon ran after him, but it was a lost cause. Casey was gone.

No. He's not gone, Brandon told himself. *He's just hiding again, and he's just gotten better at it. He's* not *gone.*

And so he kept looking.

Kikko kept running the line from that American movie in his head: *They have no idea, 'cause you're Baretta and you're totally cool.* He had no idea why someone named after a pistol meant being cool, but Kikko really liked that line. And it helped him get through this.

Derek had made it sound simple when he explained it to Kikko and Naru. "Look, all you gotta do is toss the sack into the truck when Marc and Mal ain't lookin'. Soon's it goes, we'll nab our little prize."

Of course, Derek never mentioned the nerves, or the fact that Kikko's stomach would threaten to return his lunch.

Just stay cool. Be calm.

Forcing himself to look as nonchalant as he possibly could, he carefully shifted the burlap sack from his left to his right shoulder—he didn't want to break the bottle too soon—and continued ambling casually toward the truck.

The sack was full of potassium chlorate and sugar. In and of itself, the mixture wouldn't do much, but also in the sack was a sealed glass bottle filled with gasoline and sulphuric acid. Kikko had to toss the sack into the truck hard enough to break the bottle. It would take a few minutes for the chemical reaction to take place, but when it did, there would be an explosion big enough to start a small fire on the truck—which Derek had planted there earlier, drained of gasoline—and draw the two cops' attention. Marc and Mal looked spooked enough to go apeshit over the explosion, and would be too distracted to notice Derek stealing the big lizard.

At least, that was the theory.

Kikko had considered asking Derek where he got all this stuff—most people didn't have sacks full of potassium chlorate, not to mention sulphuric acid, just laying around—but then decided he didn't want to know.

Waiting for Mal and Marc to not be looking at the truck proved fairly straightforward—they never looked at the truck. They spent all their time either looking at each other, engaged in deep conversation, or staring at the cage.

They were, in fact, looking at the cage when Kikko passed by the truck and tossed the sack in.

From this point, nonchalance went straight out the window. Derek was vague as to how long it would take the chemical reaction to take place, and Kikko wanted as much distance between him and the truck as he could get.

Kikko walked as fast as he could without actually running away from the truck. He made it to one of the shacks that lined the beach, and moved around behind it, holding his breath.

He let out the breath after the back of the truck exploded in a plume of fire.

Malau's pier was situated on a portion of the coastline that jutted out from the rest of the island's borders. That made it a more convenient port, but it also meant that there were two blind curves in which boats could hide and come upon the pier unannounced. Normally, this wasn't much of an issue, as people rarely needed to sneak up on the pier itself.

Today was not a normal day. As soon as Mal and Marc ran to the truck, shotguns in hand, to investigate, Derek brought his trawler around the bend and into sight. As soon as Kikko saw him, he ran toward the pier.

As Derek put the boat behind the cage, Kikko grabbed the ropes and moored it. Naru had a pair of bolt cutters and was trying to detach the lizard cage from the pier—a task made more difficult by the creature thrashing about inside. *Christ, can't the stupid animal see that we're trying to free it? I mean, okay, we're just going to sell it to some Indonesian guy, but he doesn't know that.*

Kikko went over to the top of the cage as Derek lowered the winch that they had set up earlier. At the end of the winch was a hook, which should, Derek said, fit on the top of the cage.

Just as Kikko grabbed the hook and put it between rungs on the cage, Naru finally broke the chain.

The creature started thrashing even more now. Kikko jumped back from the cage, landing on the pier.

"Kikko!"

At Naru's call, Kikko turned to look at his friend who was gazing down at the cage, which Derek was now raising out of the water with the winch. Kikko followed

Naru's gaze and he felt his lunch started to crawl up to his throat again.

The cage door had swung open.

Oh, shit.

Be cool. Be like Baretta. Stay calm.

Amazingly, the lizard hadn't seemed to notice that it had achieved a means of freedom. It was still jumping around, trying to attack the top of the cage, as if that would make a difference.

"Derek!" Kikko called out. He surreptitiously pointed at the cage, half convinced that the creature would see him if he pointed more overtly.

Derek followed Kikko's finger to see the open cage. "Bloody hell." He eased the winch's lever to a halt, ceasing its ascent. "Naru, go close it."

Naru's eyes went wide. Kikko couldn't blame his friend for that reaction, and he was about to object when Derek interrupted.

"Don't worry, Kikko and I will distract the beast."

Oh, we will, will we? Kikko thought, but said nothing. He leapt up onto the boat—it was probably safer there, anyhow—and positioned himself so he was facing the back end of the cage. He started whistling and jeering at the monster. Next to him, Derek did the same.

Kikko couldn't even remember what he yelled out after the words left his mouth. He was running on autopilot. *This is nuts. This is absolutely nuts. We're going to die because Derek wanted to try to steal a big lizard.*

Out of the corner of his eye, he saw Naru slowly closing the cage door.

Okay, maybe we're not going to die.

Then the cage squeaked on its hinges.

It was a small sound, and yet it seemed to Kikko as if it was loud enough to wake the dead. The lizard must have heard the sound, because it turned around.

Toward the open door.

And looked right at Naru.

Kikko swore that the lizard and Naru actually exchanged a glance. The idea was ridiculous, of course— it was just a dumb animal—but for just a moment it seemed as if some kind of understanding had passed between them. Kind of like the lizard saying, *You screwed up, pal*, and Naru saying, *Yup*.

Then the creature attacked Naru.

Though the moment between the squeak and the creature moving on Naru seemed to take forever, the subsequent several moments went very fast indeed. Kikko only remembered them as snapshots. Naru screaming. Derek leaping down toward the creature. Kikko jumping right behind Derek. Naru's blood flying through the air. The creature noticing Derek and Kikko's approach. Naru still screaming. The creature tossing Naru aside. The creature swimming into the open ocean. Derek grabbing one of his harpoon guns. Kikko remembering asking Derek why on Earth he thought he'd need harpoon guns and Derek saying, "Just in case, mate, just in case." Derek firing the harpoon gun.

Then time moved at a more normal pace as Derek dropped the spent projectile weapon and ran with Kikko to help Naru onto the boat. For a third time, Kikko had to fight down the urge to throw up. Even that American photographer hadn't been this badly messed up.

Kikko and Naru had grown up together. They had gone to Malau Elementary School together, gotten thrown off the school volleyball team together, gotten their fishing licenses together, gotten arrested by Chief Movita for illegal use of fireworks together, gotten hired by Derek together.

And now Naru was a bloody mess on Derek's boat. Kikko couldn't stand to look at it, so he turned away and looked over the starboard side of the boat.

The water, oddly, was red. Blood red. At first Kikko

thought it was Naru's blood. *But no, he was on the other side of the boat. Which means...*

"Blood. Hey, Derek, the water's full of blood over here. You hit it." Even to Kikko himself, his voice sounded like a robot's.

"Bloody wonderful," Derek muttered while starting the boat's motor.

Kikko looked up at the noise of the motor gunning. "What the hell're you doing?"

"Gettin' outta here before Mal and Marc get wise to us." He backed the boat away from the pier.

"Derek, we've gotta get him to the clinic, he's *dying!*"

Without looking at Kikko, focused as he was on steering the boat, Derek replied, "And while we take him to the clinic, what happens when they notice my boat sittin' next to the empty cage, hey? Then what?"

"But—"

"Instead of sittin' there and yellin' at me for makin' sense, why don't you grab the first-aid kit and do somethin' useful?"

That brought Kikko up short. He leapt up onto the upper level of the boat, reached under the small bench for the first-aid kit, then hopped back down to the deck and Naru's prone form.

"Naru'll keep for an hour or two—give a chance for the heat to blow over. I told a couple of people we were goin' out by Tobi, so we'll tell 'em somethin' happened out there and we got back here quick as we could."

"Right," Kikko said, not really focusing on Derek's words as he applied bandages to the rips and tears in Naru's skin. *Be cool. Stay calm. It's only the best friend you ever had in a bloody mess. Nothing to panic about.*

He wished he could believe it.

NINE

Paul hadn't wanted to say anything specific to Jack, but he was starting to get very worried.

They had spent over an hour looking for Brandon. It rarely took this long to find anyone on Malau, and the fact that no one they asked had seen him all day either was even more cause for concern.

Of course, it's possible that he's hiding on purpose. That certainly tracked with his other odd behavior over the last couple of days.

Paul met up with Jack at the end of one of the "roads"—paving had never really caught on here—near the jungle.

"Any luck?" he asked.

Jack shook his head. "No. I can't imagine where he would have gotten to. It's almost like he's deliberately trying to avoid me."

Paul laughed. "I was just thinking—" He cut himself off, as his eyes fell on the jungle.

Then it hit him. *Hiding. Jungle. Duh.* Like everyone here, he knew the story of the day that the U.S. Marines liberated the island from Japanese rule—a bunch of people hid in the jungle to avoid the fighting.

"We haven't checked the jungle," he said to Jack.

"Why would he go in there?"

"I dunno," Paul said, "but we did find him there the night we brought Ghidrah down, and if he was in there, it'd explain why no one's seen him."

Jack nodded. "C'mon."

Here I go again, Paul thought. *I think I've spent more time in this jungle in the last couple of days than I have in all the years I've lived here.* Paul hated the jungle. He preferred the wide-open spaces of the beach—or of back home in California. The idea of being where he couldn't see the sky just did not appeal.

They plowed their way through the foliage, crying out Brandon's name every couple of seconds.

To Paul's amazement and relief, Brandon actually responded, running up in front of them. He looked like hell—his eyes were red, as if he'd been crying, and his clothes were streaked with dirt and mud.

"Brandon—what were you doing—are you okay?" The words fell out of Jack's mouth in a jumble.

The boy started to talk, then stopped, then started again.

Paul prompted, "What is it, Brandon? What happened?"

Finally, Brandon said, "I had a baby creature—and I lost him."

Jack's jaw fell open. "You *what*?"

"Just like the one at the cove, but this big." He held hands up about three feet apart.

Suddenly, everything clicked into place for Paul. Brandon's questions, his concerns about the fate of the creatures, and why he was in the jungle when they nailed the big guy. *And it fits that there'd be a baby, since we already found the mother.*

"He likes cheese puffs," Brandon added, and Paul resisted the urge to giggle at the non sequitur.

"Where did you find him?" Jack asked, sounding understandably stunned. "*When* did you find him? Today?"

"Uh, no." Brandon looked down shamefacedly. Paul figured he knew why—Brandon had obviously been hoarding this baby lizard for a couple of days. "The day you went on the plane." At Jack's shocked reaction, Brandon quickly added, "I *wanted* to tell you—I *started* to tell you, but you said you couldn't stop him from being killed. I thought I could."

Once before, Paul had mused on Jack Ellway's generally even temper, and he hoped that that would hold true now. *Whatever you do, Jack, don't blow up at the kid.*

To the reporter's relief, he didn't. Instead, Jack crouched down so that he was of even height with his son and put his hands on Brandon's shoulders. Gently, he said, "Brandon, you and me—we're all we've got. We need to trust each other."

The boy didn't say anything in response, but he did look Jack in the eye, then, after a moment, smiled.

Thank God for that, Paul thought. *The question is, what happened to the baby?*

"We need to get back," Jack said.

"What about Casey?"

Jack laughed at that. "Casey, huh?"

"Well, he kinda reminded me of him."

At Paul's quizzical look, Jack explained: "Brandon had a dog named Casey. In any case, Bran, we need to get out of here and somewhere safe. This place is probably already crawling with Marines right now."

"Huh?" Brandon said.

"Uh, a lot has happened today, Brandon," Jack said, and he started to explain the day's events.

Paul tuned the conversation out. He was thinking about his front-page article on this little phenomenon, and now it just took on a new wrinkle. *An entire family of big lizards. The mind boggles. And if Jack's right, they're the result of human stupidity. How many more of those things are out there, anyhow?*

And another thought: *Cheese puffs?*

Colonel Wayne surveyed the beach and was happy with what he saw. Alfa company and Bravo, a reinforced rifle company, had almost finished setting up along the main beach, from which they planned to release the nine-foot lizard. The searchlights were all up on the edge of the beach for when it got dark—Malau's paucity of tall buildings and streetlights meant the island was almost pitch black above twenty feet—and a weapons perimeter just ahead of the lights would be all set within a few minutes.

Wayne saw two privates named Radysh and Schleiben checking over the sights on a one-oh-one recoilless rifle, which was mounted on a Hummer. *Just the thing for giant reptiles*, Wayne thought dryly.

Closer by, Privates Roman and Zimmerman were likewise checking over their own weapons—fifty-calibre machine guns. The pair were talking, not yet having noticed the colonel's presence.

"This is probably just a drill, right?" said Roman, the taller of the two. "I mean, it can't be a real situation."

"I don't know," said Zimmerman. "It doesn't feel like a drill."

"But it's too weird to be real, right?" Roman insisted.

Wayne smiled to himself and decided to let his presence be known. "Is there a problem here?"

They both shot to attention. "No sir!" they said in unison.

"Good. Carry on."

"Yes sir!" they said, and then returned to their work without further comment.

Wayne kept walking. The rumors had, of course, spread

like wildfire. Under other circumstances, the colonel would move to quash them, but he could hardly do that when the rumors were, in fact, absolutely correct—most of them, anyhow.

The reactions varied. Some dismissed the talk of giant reptiles as ridiculous, and got on with their work. Some believed every word of it, and did their work so as to be prepared. And others didn't care one way or the other, but did their work as they were told. The common factor, of course, was that, no matter what, they followed orders. They were Marines, after all, and Wayne took a certain pride in the fact that his Marines were damn good ones.

He saw President Moki and Chief Movita conversing at the edge of the beach, and Wayne moved over to join them.

"Ah, Colonel," the president said upon noticing Wayne's approach. "I see the preparations are going well."

"Yes. How's the citizenry handling it?"

"Apprehensive, but your people have been very courteous and understanding. I appreciate the fact that you haven't turned this into the stereotype of a military operation."

Wayne smiled wryly. "I've always been one to avoid the stereotypes, Mr. President."

Movita asked, "Has there been any news of the other two photographers in Askegren's picture?"

"Not that I've heard," Wayne said, shaking his head. "I've got people looking into it, though."

The chief didn't seem to notice Wayne's answer, as his attention was focused on something on the beach. "What the hell—?"

Wayne turned to see Ralph Hale running toward them. Breathlessly, he cried out, "We went to get the nine-footer—it's gone! It escaped from its cage."

"How the *hell* did that happen?" Wayne asked angrily

"Weren't Marc and Mal guarding the thing?" Movita asked Hale.

Hale nodded. "Yes, but they got sidetracked by a truck blowin' up. They figured that was a diversion, seein' as how the chains tethering the nine-footer's cage to the pier were cut."

"Damn," Wayne muttered.

"This means the giant could appear anywhere," Moki said.

"Or it might not show up at all," Hale said. "It's possible that whoever freed the beast has done our job for us."

Wayne shook his head. "Yeah, but since we didn't get to track the thing, we have no way of knowing." He unclipped the PRC from his belt. "Attention squadron leaders, this is Colonel Wayne. Second squadron, reposition to town area. Third squadron reposition to rocky coast. Fourth squadron reposition to small beach. Fifth to jungle area. Clear *all* coastal areas of civilians. Perimeter must now cover the *entire* island, not just main beach, repeat, perimeter must cover the entire island." He replaced the PRC and was about to ask Hale if he knew who was responsible for this, when he saw that Ellway and Bateman were returning—with a small kid in tow, presumably the missing son. *Well, at least something's gone right*, Wayne thought bitterly.

"The nine-footer's gone," Hale said as Ellway and the others approached, "escaped from its cage."

"Oh, my God," Ellway said.

"How the hell did *that* happen?" Bateman asked. Wayne snorted, wondering what it meant that he and the reporter both had the exact same reaction.

"It was deliberate," Hale said. "Someone distracted Marc and Mal, then cut the chain and let the bugger loose."

Ellway turned to the chief. "You don't think Derek—?"

Movita shook his head. "I doubt it. He wanted to sell the thing, he wouldn't have let it out of its cage."

The kid—*what was his name*, Wayne thought, *Brian?*—said, "So now they're both gone."

Wayne perked up at that. "Excuse me—'both'? Both what?"

"It turns out that there's a baby floating around too, Colonel," Ellway said. "Brandon found him a couple of days ago."

Throwing up his hands, Wayne said, "Oh, this just gets better and better."

"He's only three feet long, he's harmless."

"I don't care if he's three inches long, you should've told me about him."

"I didn't *know* about him," Ellway said. "Brandon only just told *me* a few minutes ago."

Brandon spoke up then. "I thought if people knew about him, they'd try to kill him. I—I didn't want him to get hurt."

Wayne sighed. He could hear the ambient noise level around him rising as his people moved to expand the perimeter and keep the civilians calm. Not far away, he could hear one of his people cautioning some Malauans to move inland. He had a bad feeling about all of this.

He looked down at Ellway's kid and said gently, "Son, you should've said something."

"I'm sorry, but I wasn't sure what would happen to him. I wanted him to be safe. He hasn't hurt anybody."

Wayne was about to respond when he noticed a change in the ambient noise. It was louder in the direction Hale had just come from. *The direction of the pier*, he remembered.

Then he heard screams.

Then he saw the head.

"My God," Ellway said.

"Whoa," Bateman said.

When he and his friend Andy had snuck out to see monster movies when they were kids, Christopher Wayne had always found it impossible to take the monsters seriously because they looked so *fake*. "Why're they all panicking?" he would ask Andy. "I mean, it's just *pâpier-maché*, right?" They made more fearsome creatures in art class.

Seeing the nine-footer in the cage hadn't mentally prepared Wayne for this. Something about being placed in a cage made the animal seem one step removed from reality. And the photograph hadn't had much of an impact, either. Photos, after all, could be faked. There were computer programs out there that could easily create a convincing photograph of a giant lizard menacing a motorboat just by digitally grafting a closeup of a small lizard onto the image of a motorboat.

Now, though...

A huge creature that towered over the tallest tree on the island was now visible by the pier. It reminded the colonel mostly of pictures of *Tyrannosaurus rex* that his nephew Howie had all over his bedroom wall, except the arms were much longer—probably long enough to work as forelegs, though the thing wasn't close enough for Wayne to see its legs yet.

All these thoughts went through Colonel J. Christopher Wayne's head in one second. It took him another second to realize that Big Mama Lizard was heading straight for the center of town. Unholstering his nine-millimeter sidearm, the colonel ran toward the town. Bateman, Ellway, Movita, and the others were on his heels.

As he ran, he whipped out his PRC. Under any other circumstances, he would trust his people not to panic. But the Corps trained you for dealing with normal-sized human foes, not forty-foot reptilian ones. So he barked the order that would otherwise have been redundant: "No one fires till I give the order!"

Damn, damn, damn, he thought as he saw the sheer panic in the streets as Malauans and tourists all scurried through the streets, some gawking at the monster as it came closer, others running in blind panic. *I should've evac'd the island the minute I got here.*

Finally, he was close enough to get a good look at Big Mama. His theory about the legs were almost right—the arms were a bit shorter than the legs, but not much. And she was definitely forty feet from head to tail, though she only stood about twenty-five feet above the ground thanks to being all leaned forward. *Actually, she's leaning more than a* T. rex *would.*

He shook his head. *Let Ellway handle the analysis.* Right now, his concerns were more immediate.

Wayne noticed that Big Mama was moving slowly and deliberately. Unlike the movie monsters of his youth, she didn't seem interested in crushing buildings or people—indeed, she was going out of her way not to step on anything other than solid ground.

Taking up position behind Manny's Fine Food and Spirits, Wayne noted that his own people had moved into position within weapons range of Big Mama, but not actually in her path. He silently praised the company commanders. *Maybe we'll be lucky and she'll just walk across the island and go back into the sea.*

Big Mama ambled casually through the center of town, for all the world like a tourist checking out the sites—except, of course, that most of the sites only came up to her middle.

She got close to where Roman and Zimmerman had taken up position, near a small grocery store. They both had their fifty-calibres out and ready. *Guess it's not too weird to be real, huh, Roman?* Wayne thought at his subordinate.

For some reason, Big Mama changed direction. Now she was headed in the general direction of the two privates.

Wayne looked at the pair—and his heart froze.

They didn't look like Marines. They looked like a couple of scared kids—like the grunts back in 'Nam who would lose it and start shooting at bushes that rustled. They looked like they were about to panic.

Marines weren't supposed to panic.

Even as Wayne raised the PRC to his lips, Roman started firing.

"Hold your fire!" Wayne screamed even as Zimmerman followed suit and also unloaded his machine gun.

The colonel wasn't sure what depressed him more—that Roman and Zimmerman disregarded the order and kept firing, or that the bullets seemed to have no effect on Big Mama whatsoever. She swatted the air like she was being menaced by mosquitoes—and, Wayne realized, mosquitoes would have about as much impact—then turned on her attackers. She slashed at Roman, who was literally cut in two by Big Mama's talons.

Zimmerman continued firing, now screaming, looking for all the world like Rambo. Colonel Wayne hated Rambo even more than he hated the tropics.

Big Mama stumbled for a moment, but steadied herself with her tail. Unfortunately, that action brought the tail smashing down into the one-story grocery store. Wayne heard screams from inside it.

Then Big Mama brought one massive claw down on Zimmerman, crushing him in one fluid motion.

An old man ran out of what was left of the grocery store and tried to get away. Wayne couldn't tell if Big Mama stepped on him deliberately, or if he was just in the way as she moved forward, and ultimately it didn't matter.

That did it. The gloves were off. His people had more

fifty-calibres, eighty-one-millimeter mortars, and three one-oh-ones on Hummers. It was going to take all of them to bring this thing down—and it needed to be brought down, Ellway's concerns notwithstanding. Big Mama was now a killer and needed to be dealt with.

"Weapons free," he said into the PRC, "say again, *weapons free*."

The air filled with the sound of explosions.

Unfortunately, all that weaponry, some of which had been used effectively as anti-tank and anti-aircraft weapons since the Second World War, had precisely no effect as anti-big-lizard weapons. They were doing a number on the local flora, fauna, and buildings, but all they served to do was drive Big Mama toward the coast.

Within minutes, she had retreated through a couple of trees and buildings and back into the water.

His people immediately moved into action, assisted by Chief Movita's people, getting the people to safety and the fires under control.

As Wayne surveyed the action, Ellway approached, along with President Moki, Chief Movita, Hale, and Bateman. Ellway's kid was there, too, but he hung back.

"This wasn't necessary," Ellway said without preamble. "None of this was necessary."

Just at the moment, Wayne had absolutely no patience for Ellway's self-righteous bullshit. "I just lost two men, Mister Ellway, not to mention dozens of injured civilians."

"I'm sorry," he said, and to Wayne's surprise, he sounded like he meant it, "I'm really sorry, but the creature wasn't attacking. It was defending itself."

Bateman said, "This all could've been averted if people had been informed—"

"Please," the president interrupted before Wayne could respond to Bateman's idiotic comment, "there is no time for this."

"Exactly," the colonel said. "It could come back at any moment. First thing I'm doing is ordering the evacuation of all civilians."

Hale's jaw fell open, something Wayne had never actually seen anyone do in real life before. "You're gonna have boats out there with that giant creature loose?"

"No, we'll use helicopters," Wayne said, wondering if Hale really thought the colonel was that stupid.

Movita said, "There are a thousand people—"

"That's why we've gotta start *now*," Wayne interrupted. "If the creature attacks again—"

Ellway then interrupted Wayne. "We can prevent another attack."

"You said that before," Wayne said, hoping he sounded as dubious as he felt.

"And I would've been right, if the nine-footer hadn't gotten loose. But there's another one, a baby. If we find it, we can use it as a lure."

Hale added, "Colonel, these creatures are an extraordinary scientific discovery."

Wayne thought about it. He also thought about the fact that Big Mama hadn't actually done any damage until after Roman fired on her. *Pity he and Zimmerman are dead, otherwise I would've had them in Leavenworth so fast their heads would've spun.* And he thought about those old monster movies, and how they always had a bloodthirsty military guy in them who came across as a complete moron.

He sighed. "And I don't want to be remembered as the guy who destroyed them." He looked at the two scientists. "Do whatever you can to prevent that thing from coming back. Because if it attacks again, I may have no choice but to kill it."

Waiting an hour to bring Naru in to the clinic worked out better than Derek could possibly have hoped. As he was pulling the trawler into its usual dock, he caught sight of the super-giant economy-size version of the nine-footer tramping through the island. Within five minutes, the sounds of a small war could be heard from the center of town, and then the monstrosity retreated to the sea.

"C'mon," he said to Kikko, "let's get him up to the clinic."

"Oh, *now* you give a damn?" Kikko said harshly.

"Look, mate, if we took him in when he got hurt, we'd be in Movita's cell right now. But who's gonna question somebody torn up by a big lizard now, yeah?"

"Fine, whatever," Kikko said, gingerly picking the now-bandaged Naru up off the deck into a firefighter's carry.

They made a beeline for the clinic—or as much of a beeline as they could, given all the people scurrying about. *Where the hell did all these troops come from?* Derek wondered. He hadn't been on shore since that morning when he left that clapped-out old truck of his for Kikko to blow up by the beach. *Looks like Manny called in the Marines. Christ almighty, that's just what we need—more bleedin' yanks stickin' their nose in our business.*

When they got to the clinic, they found that the place was already pretty full. People with pressure bandages, people wearing casts, people with bruises—and that was just in the waiting room. Most of them, however, gasped at the sight of Naru, who was now covered in first-aid bandages that barely did the job of staunching the bleeding.

Doctor Hart came out to see what all the fuss was about. She looked somewhat taken aback by the severity of Naru's injuries. "My God," she said, "what *happened* to Naru?"

Derek had spent the past ten minutes rehearsing the speech. "It was all so fast, with the big monster stomping around and people carrying on. I don't know, suddenly Naru was screaming, and—"

"Never mind," Hart interrupted, motioning for her nurse to bring in a gurney. "Let's get him onto the examination table."

The nurse wheeled the gurney in. Kikko gently put his friend down on it, then the nurse and Hart brought him into the exam room. Kikko tried to follow, but Hart held him back. "We'll let you know how he's doing, okay?"

Kikko looked disappointed, but nodded and said, "Okay."

Derek couldn't find a seat in the waiting room, and besides, he felt a sudden urge for a cigarette. Since he couldn't smoke in the clinic anyhow, he went out onto the verandah.

Kikko came out as he lit the cigarette. "Nice job. Covered your ass real good."

"Both our arses, mate."

"Don't 'mate' me, Derek," Kikko snapped. This took Derek aback—he'd known Kikko for years, and he'd never snapped at anyone in all that time that Derek could remember. "If he dies—"

"He *won't* die. He's in good hands."

Kikko seemed to deflate. "I hope so." Then he turned and sat on one of the verandah chairs.

Derek stared out at the chaos of the island. He heard helicopters, then looked up and saw a great number of them.

One of the military blokes walked by. "Hey, soldier," he called out, "what's goin' on?"

"Evac," the man said. "We're gettin' all civilians off the island as fast as possible." He looked at Derek. "You got family in the clinic?"

"Kinda, yeah."

"Well, as soon as the doc gives the okay, we'll be moving all the patients outta there. They'll be put in the hospital on Kalor. You two should get over to the airfield."

"We're not leaving till we know what happened to Naru," Kikko said.

"I'm kinda responsible for him, so we need to stick around," Derek said.

"Suit yourselves. Your funeral if Ma Gator comes back, though." And with that, the Marine walked off.

Bleedin' idiot, Derek thought as he took a drag on the cigarette. *Like we're goin' anywhere.* He wasn't going to leave until he knew that Naru would live. He owed his employee that much.

It pained him to see Kikko's concern—pained him mainly because he didn't share it to anything like the same degree. Oh, he liked Naru well enough, and the three of them made a good team and all that, but Kikko and Naru were best friends. They had a bond Derek had never had with anyone.

After almost an hour and several more cigarettes, Hart came out.

Kikko almost flew out of his chair. "Is Naru gonna be all right? Good as new?"

Hart sighed. "Good as new I can't promise. But he'll pull through, that's the main thing."

"Poor bloke," Derek muttered, wondering if perhaps Naru could have been "as good as new" if Derek hadn't insisted on waiting before bringing him in. *All my fault*, he thought.

"Why would you say that?" Hart asked.

Damn, didn't realize I'd said that out loud. He thought quickly. "That's the way I am," he said with what he hoped was a casual shrug, "taking responsibility for everything."

The doctor looked like she was going to say something, but Kikko, bless him, spoke up. "Can I look in on Naru?"

"Sure," Hart said with a nod. "He's sedated, so he

won't know you're there," she added as she led him inside.

"He'll know," Kikko said, sounding very sure of himself.

Derek flicked his cigarette onto the verandah. "Stuffed," he muttered, "it's all stuffed. Dammit."

Jack had to admit to being impressed with Colonel Wayne. He had created an image in his head of a cigar-chomping luantic who would view Jack as a weak-kneed scientist who didn't know how to get things done. *Of course, that image was of a white guy, too*, he thought with no small embarrassment. But Wayne had been very reasonable—he didn't listen to everything Jack said, of course, and had his own agenda, but he took Jack seriously as a consultant, which was frankly more than he was expecting.

He was saying to Wayne: "It's unlikely the giant creature would return to this part of the island where it was attacked."

"Agreed—up to a point, anyhow. Let's face it, we don't have much of a basis to form a behavior pattern."

"True," Jack conceded.

"In any case, we'll reposition to the more secluded beach areas and wait."

Brandon arrived then, armed with a bag of cheese puffs. Apparently the baby creature really loved the junk food, a fact Jack found terminally depressing. *Bad enough Brandon eats that crap*. The hope was that the puffs would serve as a lure.

"All set?" Jack asked. At Brandon's nod, he said, "Let's go find your little friend." He was about to set off when something occurred to him. They still didn't know the final fate of the adolescent—the one Jack had thought of as Superlizard, a name that no longer seemed applicable. He turned back to the colonel. "I don't know whether the nine-footer is back in the water or still on the island. Can you spare a couple of men?"

Wayne considered this. "All right," he said after a moment. He turned to one of his people—a sergeant, based on the stripes on his arm. "Get Radysh and Schleiben over here. And get Ellway a radio." As the sergeant moved off, presumably to fetch the two people, Wayne turned to Jack and said very slowly and clearly, "Keep me informed."

"Thank you for letting me try this," Jack said, meaning it.

"I'm hoping you succeed. I hope it very much," Wayne said, sounding like he meant it, too.

Within minutes, two Marines had arrived, one of them providing a radio for Jack. He collected Paul and Doctor Hale, and then the five of them followed Brandon into the jungle.

In addition to a pair of rifles, Privates Radysh and Schleiben carried large flashlights.

Jack had been somewhat distracted the last time he came into the jungle at night, so it wasn't until now that he appreciated how loud the place was when the sun went down. The noise was matched only by the sounds of mortar fire from when the Marines went after the mother lizard.

Unlike their two fellow privates, Radysh and Schleiben didn't panic, nor seem overly jumpy. *Wish I could say the same*, Jack thought. *I'm half expecting the nine-footer to come leaping out at me.* Next to him, Paul and Doctor Hale looked equally apprehensive.

But Brandon, bless his little heart, didn't look at all fazed by the jungle noises or the very real danger. He looked more worried than scared, and Jack suspected that it was on behalf of the baby lizard. *Casey*, he remembered. *He named it after that puppy we got him—Lordy, that was six years ago.* While he was mildly annoyed

with Brandon for keeping Casey's existence a secret, it
may have turned out to be a blessing in disguise. If they'd
known about it sooner, it probably would have wound up
in a cage next to the nine-footer, and whoever released
the one would have released the other. *Now that little guy
may be the only way to keep the mother from crushing
Malau under her big feet.*

Suddenly, Brandon stopped, motioning the adults to
stop as well. The two Marines stood with perfect posture,
rifles down but ready to go at a moment's notice. Hale
and Paul just stopped and looked at Brandon, as did Jack.

Brandon seemed to be listening for something. Then
he must have heard it, because he reacted to a particular
noise, though how he could distinguish one noise from
another in this cacophany was beyond Jack. Then he
looked around at the jungle floor, peering into various
bushes and things—then he found something and moved
toward it, cheese puffs in hand.

Radysh and Schleiben moved in time with Jack right
behind him. Schleiben shined his flashlight at the area in
front of Brandon.

Jack peered into the beam, and saw a miniature vesion
of the creature that stomped across Malau earlier that
evening. The eyes were proportionately bigger and the
scales smoother, but it looked just like Big Mama, as
Colonel Wayne had taken to calling her.

However, Jack only got the briefest of gazes at Casey,
for a second after the light hit him, he dashed off into the
underbrush.

Brandon turned angrily on Schleiben and Radysh.
"You scared him! Stay back!"

Jack was worried that the two men would take
umbrage at being given orders by a twelve-year-old, but
they simply nodded and stood back, lowering their flashlights.

Satisfied that the Marines were out of the way, Brandon

got down into a crouch, clutching the bag of cheese puffs for dear life, and moved into the foliage where Casey had slipped off. He rustled the bag a couple of times, then gripped it by both sides and pulled it open. Reaching in, he took out a handful of the vile foodstuff—*his hands are going to get all orange*, Jack thought with an internal sigh—and held them out expectantly.

Part of Jack Ellway refused to believe that any marine creature could possibly be interested in eating food that was laced with more preservatives and chemicals than the average pesticide.

Then he realized what he was thinking. *Artificial chemicals were responsible for these creatures' existence.*

He decided he didn't want to examine that thought very closely.

Besides which, he didn't have the opportunity, as Casey actually poked his little head out and started munching on the puffs, eating out of Brandon's hand exactly the same way a dog or cat would. *Remarkable.*

Slowly, very slowly, Brandon carefully moved backward, leading Casey out of the undergrowth. When Casey finished the puffs, Brandon turned around and started walking normally. Casey stuck behind him, following just like an obedient dog. *Geez, he's got that thing trained better than the puppy.* The baby lizard's namesake had never been an especially obedient dog. *But this Casey is.*

Jack was moved by the sight. *A boy and his lizard. Who'da thunk it?*

The touching moment was shattered by the squawk of the radio that Jack had clipped to his belt.

Casey stopped walking, and froze in his tracks, obviously not sure what to make of this alien noise.

Cursing himself for not doing it sooner, Jack turned down the volume on the radio and put it to his mouth. He heard Wayne's filtered voice say, "Have you found anything?"

Really lousy timing, Colonel, Jack thought. But then, Jack had been asked to keep Wayne informed, and Jack hadn't been doing that.

Jack whispered into the speaker: "We found the baby."

"I can't hear you," said Wayne's voice, still distressingly loud despite the volume being turned down.

Speaking a bit louder, Jack said, "We've got the baby. We're on our way."

"Give me a time," the colonel said.

How the hell should I know? Jack bit back the retort, took a breath and said, "Soon. We're on our way."

Brandon looked down at Casey, then started walking. Casey, having apparently decided that the noise was nothing to be concerned about, again followed alongside him.

How about that, Jack thought, *we just might pull this off.*

TEN

"**W**hen that judge gave me the choice to go to jail or join the Marines, I should've given it a little more thought."

T.J. White rolled his eyes. *Why the hell did I have to be partnered with Jace?* he asked whatever gods or generals controlled such things. Actually, it was neither god nor general who decreed that the pair of them be assigned to the two ground-to-air missle launchers and stationed on the Malau beach waiting for the Mother of All Lizards to make a return engagement—it was Sergeant Szabo.

Not that Harold "Jace" Jason was a bad person or a bad Marine, it's just that he never tired of reminding people of the fact that he was in the Marines only because it beat the alternative of jail time. It especially irked T.J. since the little incident with that general. T.J. was the only black man in a squad that was run by a white sergeant and also included eight white men and two Asian men. Some four-star or other had come to inspect the troops, and when he got to their squadron, he mentioned that he'd heard that one member of the squad was a convicted criminal serving his sentence with the Corps. The general then made a beeline for T.J. and assumed that he was the felon.

To this day, it rankled on T.J.

However, it didn't rankle nearly as much as the fact that he'd spent his entire tour sitting on his ass. Not that being a Marine meant anything other than constant work, but still....

"We're havin' *action*, man," he said to Jace. "I got to thinkin' we'd never have action."

"Look, man, I saw enough action in Baltimore," Jace said, pronouncing it "Bahl-mer."

"What, you joined the Corps to *relax?*"

Jace grinned. "Naw, I just figured it'd be better than some lifer decidin' I'd make a good squeeze."

T.J. was about to make a comment along the lines of how good a squeeze he'd make, but then he noticed something happening—or, rather, noticed something not happening. One of the searchlights stopped moving. T.J. tensed up; next to him, Jace did likewise.

Out of the corner of his eye, T.J. saw Colonel Wayne raise his binoculars. If the colonel saw anything, he didn't react to it. *Not that he would*, T.J. thought, and looked back out at the ocean. He couldn't see anything in the searchlight's beam.

Turning around to look at the searchlight operator, T.J. saw the private struggle with the light for a minute, then move it again.

Great, the stupid thing was just stuck.

Wayne relaxed and set his binoculars back down. Then he started pacing the beach.

Several ice ages came and went, though T.J.'s watch insisted it had only been a minute or so. In direct contrast to the constant noise that had been the hallmark of this operation since they first landed on Malau—between setting up and routing civilians around, not to mention the chaos of the cleanup after the Mother of All Lizards' attack—it was now very quiet.

If Jace turns to me and says, "It's real quiet," figuring I'll say, "Yeah, too quiet," I'm gonna shoot him *with the damn missle launcher.*

So when the water started to churn, T.J. noticed.

Wayne was standing right behind T.J. and Jace's position when the noise started. Again, the colonel brought his binoculars to his eyes.

Besides the water, there was something else: a kind of low rumble.

Then a massive head broke through the surface, followed by the rest of the body of the Mother of All Lizards.

Damn, T.J. thought, *she came back*. He couldn't imagine why, given the reception she got before. *Then again, it's not like we hurt her or nothing*. That's why Wayne had ordered the missle launchers set up. They couldn't very well have used them in the middle of town, but on a beach deserted of all save Marines, they'd work just fine.

At least T.J. hoped they would.

The searchlights all converged, illuminating Mother as she came out of the water and onto the beach in full forty-foot glory. *Jesus Christ, she's huge*, T.J. thought. He hadn't seen her quite this close the last time.

Behind him, the colonel spoke into his PRC. "Where are you, Ellway?"

"Close," said a scratchy voice through the speaker. "We're close."

"It's back. Say again, it's come back." Wayne sounded pretty damn calm for someone who was talking about a forty-foot reptile.

"We're coming," said the tinny voice, "we're not far."

Mother stomped across the beach. This wasn't the

casual stroll it took the last time—this was a bull-in-a-china-shop walk, a big lizard that wasn't letting anything get in her way.

"It's approaching—I can't hold off much longer!" Wayne said, now sounding much less calm.

"Please wait, we're *almost there*! I can see the lights," said the voice on the PRC. T.J. wondered who it was the colonel was talking to and what he was supposed to bring to the party.

Mother reared her head back and let out a yell.

I do not like the sound of that, T.J. thought, and started praying.

Then the creature continued her approach.

Right at T.J.

In the back of his head, Private Thomas Jefferson White knew that Mother wasn't really heading directly for him, that he was but one of many troops who just happened to be in the big lizard's way. But in the front of his head, he saw a forty-foot monstrosity bearing down right on *him*.

Our father, who art in heaven, hallowed be thy name, he thought as he heard Colonel Wayne say, "Fire!"

T.J. raised the rocket launcher to his shoulder. *Thy kingdom come, thy will be done.*

He fired.

On Earth as it is in heaven.

Next to him, Jace did likewise.

Give us this day our daily bread, and forgive us our trespasses.

Twin streaks of light shot through the air from the perimeter to the chest of the Mother of All Lizards. And, unlike the mortar, bullets, and shells of before, these actually penetrated Mother's scaly hide. She let out a nasty scream, louder, higher-pitched, and longer than the previous wail.

As we forgive those who trespass against us.

"No!" "Stop!" "No!"

T.J. saw three civilians—two adults, one kid—running toward the beach, shouting at the tops of their lungs.

And lead us not into temptation, but deliver us from evil.

The earth below T.J.'s feet shook as Mother pitched forward and collapsed in a heap on the beach with a second cry.

Amen.

It's over. I'm still alive. Thank you, God, T.J. thought, crossing himself.

Jace looked at him. "That actually *work*?"

"We're still alive, ain't we?"

Then he saw a tiny creature that was a dead ringer for Mother scampering out onto the beach, making a beeline for the giant lizard.

The baby creature got to Mother's side just as she closed her eyes for the last time.

Within a few seconds, the little kid civilian caught up with the baby and took it in his arms like it was his pet or something.

This, T.J. decided, *is just too weird.*

"Y'know," Jace said, "when that judge gave me the choice to go to jail or join the Marines, I shoulda given it a little more thought."

T.J. rolled his eyes. "Jace, *shut* up."

Jack Ellway shook his head in amazement as he examined the corpse of the forty-foot lizard. *One second she's stomping around the beach. The next second, she's falling onto the beach. Alive, dead, just like that.* He compared it to the lingering agony of Diane's bout with a brain tumor, of watching her disintegrate slowly from both the disease and the chemotherapy, then one day falling asleep and not waking up.

He wondered which was preferable.

"It's a female," he was saying, trying to keep his mind on the work rather than grisly speculations about mortality. President Moki, Chief Movita, Colonel Wayne, Doctor Hale, and Alyson all stood nearby, and Brandon sat on the sand a few feet away, Casey cradled in his arms. Wayne had ordered several searchlights to remain trained on the area, so the place was almost as well lit as it was in sunlight. "I'm sure it's the mother of the baby here," he indicated the three-footer, "and the nine-foot adolescent."

The chief asked Wayne, "Will the nine-foot creature return? Must we prepare?"

"We'll plan for it," Wayne said, "but I'm not as worried."

Of course not, Jack thought bitterly. *We've just proven it's no match for us.*

"Could there be others out there?" Hale asked. "A family—or colony?"

"I hope so," Jack said. Everyone turned to look at Jack like he had two heads after he said that. By way of explanation, he continued, "We discover three members of a brand-new species and immediately reduce it to two. We're the human predator at its worst."

"I won't play that game, Ellway," Wayne said angrily. "We did the best we could."

"That's what the predator always says."

"Look," Wayne said, "if it's a choice between that thing and human lives, it *isn't* a choice. Do you read me?"

"Oh yes, Colonel, loud and clear. If you had just waited—"

Wayne interrupted. "Between them, these two creatures have killed at least five people, maybe more. If I didn't give the order to fire, that number would have tripled."

Paul came running up before Jack could reply to this. "Well, it was inevitable. Fox News got wind of this.

They're on their way. And God knows who else is in their wake."

President Moki shook his head. "Our island will never be the same."

You ain't kidding, Jack thought, though that was true the minute the nine-footer got tangled up in the same fishing net as two women from Minnesota.

He looked at Colonel Wayne. "The carcass needs to be shipped someplace to be preserved and studied," he said in a mild tone. "I'm going to contact the National Institute of Science."

Wayne spoke in a gentle tone as well: "I have to inform the Brigadier General in Okinawa of what's going on here. In the meantime," he turned to two men wearing captain's bars, "I want this beach cleared and guarded until further notice." The two captains nodded and moved off. Wayne turned back to Jack. "We'll keep the scavengers away till I get my orders."

"Dad," Brandon said. Jack turned to see his son now standing close by, the three-footer by his side. "What's gonna happen to *him*?"

Jack considered. "Well, he seems to trust you. I guess you'll just keep looking after him for the time being." He thought about it for a moment. "We should take him back to the room and examine him. The most important thing right now is to make sure he eats."

"Who's making sure that you guys eat?" Alyson asked.

Jack hesitated, realizing that he had no idea when his last meal *was*.

Before he could reply, Alyson said, "I'll bring you some dinner, okay?"

He smiled. "Thanks."

Hale stretched his arms and announced, "I, for one, need to lie down before I fall down."

Jack grinned at that. Hale probably hadn't had a nap in as long as Jack hadn't had a meal. He put his hand on

Brandon's shoulder, and led him and Casey off toward the hotel.

Derek didn't hear about the giant monster's return until after it was all over. He had heard the commotion, and the firing of some kind of large weapon or other, but he hadn't seen any of it—the main beach wasn't visible from the clinic verandah, situated as it was behind the building.

As soon as he did hear, though, he was on tenterhooks waiting for Kikko to come out from his little visit with Naru. As soon as Kikko's head poked out of the doorway, Derek grabbed him. "C'mon," he said.

"What is it?"

"One of the soldiers that went by says they nailed the mother lizard. I wanna gander." They started walking toward the beach. "How's Naru?"

"Sedated, like the doc said," Kikko replied. "He's lucky the thing missed hitting anything important. Just shredded a lotta skin and broke a coupl'a ribs."

"That's good news, mate."

"Yeah," Kikko said, not sounding like he meant it.

Within minutes, they arrived at the beach—or, at least, the edge of it. A bunch of Marines were keeping anyone from getting too close.

Anyone, that is who actually lived on the island. Once again, Derek saw that Hale, Bateman, Ellway, and his dumb kid all got to be in where the good stuff was happening. Or had happened, in this case, since the magnificent creature that had stalked the island now lay dead on one of its beaches. "What a bloody waste," Derek muttered. "The money that could've been made from this thing...."

He thought again about that Indonesian bloke.

"The nine-footer could still be around," he whispered to Kikko. "It's wounded—might be easy to catch."

"Derek—" Kikko started.

"We'll have a look in the morning. All may not be lost."

A Marine walked up to them. "I'm sorry, but I'm afraid I'm going to have to ask you people to move along. We need to clear this entire area."

Bloody yanks, tellin' us what to do, Derek thought angrily. He was well and truly sick of that.

As he and Kikko walked away, heading back toward the trawler—if nothing else, they needed to clean Naru's blood off the deck—he noticed Ellway and his kid walking away from the massive corpse. He also noticed that the kid had something walking alongside him.

Sweet Jesus, he thought. Next to the boy walked a miniature version of the corpse, only up and walking around. *Must be another part of the family. And it isn't likely to go around disembowelling people.*

Visions of paid alimony, paid taxes, a yacht, and restaurants in Fiji danced in Derek's head.

While he was no veterinarian, Jack knew enough about animal husbandry to at least do a perfunctory examination of Casey. It lay on the floor while Jack checked it over—the no-frills Ritz only provided one desk, and it was presently laden with Jack's equipment—with Brandon also on the floor, nose-to-nose with him, feeding him cheese puffs. Jack had wanted to provide a little balance in Casey's diet by giving him some of the Iozima Ridge water and plant life he and Paul had given the nine-footer the previous day, but Brandon would hear none of it. "I already tried the usual stuff," Brandon had said. "He'll just eat cheese puffs." Jack doubted this to be completely true, but decided to indulge the boy.

"His eyes are clear, his heartbeat steady." He stood up. "It's hard to know what's normal for this guy, of course."

The examination complete, Brandon sat up and started petting Casey as if he were a dog. "He saw his mother die. That's the worst thing in the world."

Jack felt like he'd been kicked in the stomach. In the last year, he and Brandon had mostly dealt with Diane's death by not dealing with it, not talking about it, nothing. The closest he had come was the half-hearted, one-sided conversation they'd had while gathering invertebrates for the nine-footer to not eat.

Dammit, I don't even know how to deal with Diane's death. How the hell am I supposed to help him deal with it? All I've done is run away—dash off to Vancouver, run over to Hawaii, scurry away to Maine.

"Well," he said slowly, deciding to deal with the surface concern, if not the real one, "he's got you now. When you lose someone—" he hesitated "—someone who took care of you—it helps if someone's there to take over. Someone else who can love you and protect you."

Still petting Casey and not looking up at Jack, Brandon asked, "What if it's not enough?"

Ouch. "I'm afraid it's gotta be."

Brandon looked up at his father. Normally he could read his son like a book, but now Jack had no idea what was going through that twelve-year-old brain.

Suddenly, Brandon leaned over and nabbed a coconut that he had picked up on the way to the hotel. "Would you like to play with him?"

Jack just stared dumbfounded at the coconut for a moment.

"Just roll it to him."

Ah, what the hell, Jack thought. He took the proferred fruit and rolled it to Casey.

Casey got up on his hind legs and stopped the coconut's roll with his arms. Then he rolled the coconut to Brandon.

Jack couldn't help it. He laughed. The laughter felt good.

It was also infectious, as Brandon started to laugh, too, as he rolled the coconut back to Casey.

Casey, now even more perked up, rolled the coconut back to Jack.

They kept the game up for some time.

"It looked at me. Looked me in the eye. Right when my missile hit, it *knew* who was killing it."

T.J. sighed as Jace muttered. They had drawn guard duty on the Mother of All Lizard's remains for the night shift. Ever since they came on at midnight, Jace had been going on and on about the actual kill. The looking-into-the-eye bit was just the latest embellishment. Sure, T.J. had had the impression *at the time* that Mother was heading straight for him, but that was because of all the adrenaline pumping. Now that he had distance, he knew better, knew that he was just a cog in a wheel that brought the thing down.

Jace, though—he made it more personal with each retelling. In another minute, it would have been only Jace's missile, not both his and T.J.'s, that killed the creature.

All in all, T.J. was starting to get nostalgic for the rant about the choice the judge gave him.

"Will you please just shut up about it, man? You got yourself a damn fine trophy."

"I guess," Jace said.

And then he was actually quiet for a minute. T.J. almost cheered.

But it couldn't last. "Hey," Jace said, "will you take a picture of me next to it?"

I don't believe this. But before T.J. could say anything, he heard a sound.

A familiar sound.

It was like the churning and rumbling that preceded Mother's arrival on the beach earlier that night—only a helluva lot louder.

"Did you hear that?" Jace asked.

"Yeah. What was it?"

"Dunno," Jace said.

T.J. unhooked both the flashlight and the PRC from his belt and moved closer to the surf. Next to him, Jace did likewise.

Then the ground started to shake.

This actually put T.J. at ease. *They have tremors here all the time. No biggie. They've been having more of them lately, too, so it's* really *no biggie. Nothing to worry about at all.*

He believed that right up until the water started to churn.

Oh my Lord Jesus Christ, it's happening again.

Something broke through the water. Something considerably larger than the Mother of All Lizards.

Our father, T.J. thought, *who art in heaven, hallowed be thy name.*

This time, he didn't get to finish the prayer.

ELEVEN

For the second time in two days, one of the giant lizards had gone missing. Jack Ellway found it pretty difficult to credit this second disappearance. After all, the last time, all that had to be done was get a cage open, and the nine-footer could take it from there. Corpses, though, needed to be moved by something, and very few somethings could move a forty-foot-long reptile.

In fact, there was only one serious possibility.

He was once again on the beach, flanked by Paul and Doctor Hale, discussing that very possibility. A flattened area of sand was all there was to indicate that a huge creature once died on this beach. A wide swath of flattened sand led from that indentation into the sea. Jack presently crouched by the edge of the area where the mother had lain.

"So this just became a rerun of 'Father Lizard Knows Best,' or what?" Paul said.

"Something like that," Jack replied. "Look at the

impressions in the sand." He pointed to the swath. "I can't imagine what else could drag the mother out into the ocean like that."

"Not under the noses of two now-missing Marines," Hale said.

"No." He stood up straight and sighed. "We're gonna need to find this thing." He turned to Hale. "The Topex Satellite—they use that to track whales, right?"

"Yeah, among other things." The light bulb went off over Hale's head. "Not a bad idea, Jack."

Jack looked up to see Colonel Wayne and Chief Movita talking to each other, Wayne also speaking into his walkie-talkie. Beyond them, President Moki was approaching. "C'mon," he said, "let's go fill the brass in."

Upon seeing the trio's approach, Wayne lowered his radio.

"Talk to me, Ellway," Wayne said, and Jack was grateful that the colonel was still seeking his input.

"Jack, tell him what you're thinking," Hale prompted—unnecessarily, Jack thought at first, but then he noticed the fact that everyone seemed to be paying more attention after Hale spoke. Although no more a local than Jack, Hale did have a reputation behind him, and his support meant Jack would be taken more seriously.

"I speculated before that this was a family situation. I think Dad may have come to claim Mom's body."

Moki shook his head. "And so it continues."

Wayne nodded, as if he'd already thought this—*and maybe he had*, Jack thought—and started talking fast. "All right, we'll resume the evac plan. I want all civilians safely off island by nightfall."

However, Jack still had concerns. "And if there is another giant creature, what then? Shoot on sight?"

Wayne let out a loud breath through his nostrils that made him sound like a horse. Tersely, he said, "Give me a *plan*, Ellway."

"Okay," Jack said, and turned to Hale.

Taking the cue, Hale said, "We can use the Topex Satellite to locate whatever's out there. It's frequently used to track whales, so it'd be pretty easy to recalibrate it. I can have my boys at the Institute handle it."

Wayne considered this, then, "Fine, I'll arrange for an AWAC to do the same."

This took Jack aback. He had expected agreement at best, outright denial and censure at worst. Cooperation hadn't even been considered. "Good," he said, "great! Wonderful."

"Well, don't just stand there, Ellway, get to work," Wayne said, then turned his back on Jack and Hale.

Did I imagine it, or was the colonel hiding a smile?

Dismissing the thought, he and Hale started walking toward his bungalow to make the call to his institute.

"The question before us now," Hale said, "is what we do when we find the beast?"

Jack had actually been giving that matter some thought for several days. "What about luring the creature back to its home?" he asked. "We could use different sounds to attract it and to divert it."

Hale frowned. "Well, high-frequency sounds could keep it at bay, but what would attract it?"

Jack rubbed his chin. "Amphibians communicate with each other by sound. We could record the voice of the baby creature and amplify it. We'd bring the baby with us on a boat with Dad following behind, guided by speakers in the water."

Hale said, "You make it sound easy."

"Really?" Jack replied with a smile. "I think it sounds insane."

Laughing, Hale said, "Fine, once we've got the creatures home, how do we make certain they stay there?"

"Good question." Sadly, he had no idea. He looked up at the geologist. "Got an answer?"

"Not at the moment," Hale said, but he said it in a far-away voice.

Jack grinned. The geologist would probably have an idea by the time they got to his bungalow.

After they had themselves a fortifying breakfast on the trawler, Derek had sent Kikko off to find the nine-footer. A good night's sleep and breakfast must have returned Kikko's enthusiasm, because he seemed like his old self again—and was quite eager to track the creature down. Derek had given him a pair of binoculars, one of his harpoon guns, and a rope and sent him on his way.

Derek himself had been all set to do likewise, but first he wanted to get another look at the huge corpse.

He was rather surprised to find that the thing had gone missing. And this time, Derek himself had nothing to do with it. He wasn't worried about being suspected for it. In fact, he'd made an effort to strike up a brief conversation with the chief, during which Derek ascertained that Movita didn't consider Derek a suspect in that particular theft. "Probably some environmentalist nut who wants to keep all creatures in their natural habitat or something," the chief had said. Derek had made affirmative noises, then excused himself.

The big, dead lizard, though—that disappearance was cause for concern. *Unless they evacuated it in the middle of the night? But if that's so, why is Ellway standin' around with Hale and the others?*

"Excuse me, sir," said yet another bloody Marine, "I'm going to have to ask you to move along to the airfield."

"I beg your pardon?" he said.

"The airfield, sir. Colonel Wayne has ordered the evacuation of all civilians from Malau."

"Fine, of course," Derek said with all the amiability of someone who had no intention of listening. "Uh, if you don't mind my askin', what happened to the corpse?"

The Marine tensed up at that. "It was taken by person or persons unknown, sir. That's why the island's being evacuated. Now *please* move along, sir."

Bloody bastard, he thought, but smiled at the man and moved along.

But not without another glance at Ellway and the others. Noticeably absent was Ellway's kid—and the little bite-sized lizard. *Ellway probably sent the little bloke back to the hotel.*

Sniffing opportunity in the wind, he headed for the Hotel Ritz.

He arrived to see Ellway's kid sitting on the lawn behind the tiny hotel, playing with the little creature. *A boy and his bleedin' lizard. Real cute.*

Trying to look casual, and making sure there wasn't anybody else around, Derek sauntered up to the boy.

"Cute little monkey, innhe?"

Brandon glanced up at him, shrugged, and continued playing with the little monster.

"Have you given him a name? Gotta give a pet a name."

"Casey," Brandon said. "I had a dog named Casey. He got lost."

Sentimental little brat, Derek thought, but said, "Good, solid name, Casey." He crouched down, raised his hand as if to pet it, then looked at Brandon. "May I?"

Another shrug. "Whatever."

Derek petted the little thing, and it seemed to like that. At the creature's seeming happiness, Brandon actually smiled.

All right, mi'lad, time to throw the pitch. "It's a shame, what's gonna end up happening to little Casey."

Brandon's smile fell into a frown. "What do you mean?"

"It's only a matter of time before they come and take him away."

"Who?" The kid sounded indignant.

"The government. Your little friend is gonna end up in a lab somewhere, dissected like a frog."

Brandon snatched the little demon and held it to him like it was a teddy bear. "My dad wouldn't let that happen."

"Your dad's a terrific guy, kid," Derek managed to say with a straight face, "but he's got no power in this. When the military gets hold of Casey, it's off to the lab." He looked around conspiratorially, as if making sure they couldn't be overheard, then stage-whispered, "We don't have to let that happen, you and I. We can save your little friend—get him outta here before it's too late. We could take him away on my boat—all the way to Kalor, all the way to safety."

Brandon's lips twisted—he was obviously seriously considering it. "I gotta think about it," he said.

Bloody hell. "Maybe I can help you think—what's your problem with it?"

"Nothing, I just—"

Move in for the kill. "Fine, it's all settled then—right?" After a second: "Right."

"Fantastic," Derek said, clapping his hands and standing up. "You're a bright and courageous young man. Meet me at my boat in an hour. Don't forget the little monkey."

"I won't," Brandon said with a smile.

Derek smiled back, then headed back into town. *Like shootin' fish in a bleedin' barrel. Fiji, here I come.*

Kikko had figured it out during the night. It all came clear to him, so much so that it should have been obvious from the get-go.

It was learning that the large creature had been killed by the Marines that did it. It made everything just crystal-clear.

All these creatures had to die.

And so did Derek Lawson.

First things first, though. Gotta find that thing that maimed Naru and kill it. Kill it until it's dead.

He had managed to avoid the Marine patrols and work his way to the comparative seclusion of Elephant Rock. Avoiding the patrols had been easy—Kikko had been avoiding people like that all his life, whether it was the hall guards at school or Joe Movita's cops.

Besides, he had a mission to perform. Naru had sacrificed himself to show Kikko his true purpose: he had to kill the creatures.

The creatures were abominations. They deserved to die.

And so did Derek Lawson for trying to keep the abominations for himself.

And for getting Naru hurt. And almost killed.

Yes, Derek had to die.

But first the creatures.

He raised the binoculars to his eyes and scanned the rocky coast. *C'mon, you were hurt, you couldn't have gotten that far. And if you wanted to stay out of sight, this place'd be perfect.*

The guess paid off. He caught sight of a very familiar-looking reptile form, lying unmoving on Elephant Rock, blood trickling from a large gash in its leg.

"A bit under the weather, eh, big fella?" Kikko laughed a cruel laugh.

He moved closer to the creature, clambering over rocks. It was slow going, weighed down as he was with the harpoon gun, but he wasn't in a terrible rush, either. There was no one around. He could make this nice and slow. After all, the abomination had to suffer before it died.

As Kikko approached, the monster raised its head and roared. Kikko just laughed, bent over, picked up a small rock, and threw it at the creature.

The rock collided with the thing's head. It roared again, then lowered its head back to the rock.

Giggling madly, Kikko said, "Not so tough with a hole in your leg, are you?" He uncoiled the rope that he had tied around his waist. Within seconds, he'd fashioned into a noose. "The hangman cometh, big guy. And it's all going to be over for you with the snap of a neck. Or maybe I'll just stab you in the heart. Assuming you've got one, anyhow. See, I haven't figured out what'll make you suffer the most. Tough choice, y'know?" He grinned. "I know! Whichever way I don't kill you is how I'll kill Derek! Wouldn't that be just perfect? So, let's think. Noose or harpoon, noose or harpoon?"

He stopped his climb and scratched his head. Then he thrust his index finger into the air. "*I* know! I'll use the noose on you! Why, you may ask? Yes, a good question. Why? Well, you see, I want Derek to *bleed*. I want his blood to pour out all over the place like Naru's did when you clawed him. But if I'm going to do that, it means I *have* to kill you with the noose—you *do* understand, don't you? Of *course* you do. Yes indeedy."

Kikko climbed up behind the abomination. *This is going to be fun.*

Then it got dark.

It's morning. It can't get dark. And it's not cloudy.

Realizing he was now in something's shadow, he turned around.

The sky was blotted out by a ten-foot-long head with two horns on top of it.

Jesus, Mary, and Joseph. The big daddy of all abominations.

Kikko screamed.

The head leaned forward. Its teeth were numerous, looked to be razor-sharp, and were heading straight for Kikko.

He expected it to hurt.

He expected to care about this.

Neither turned out to be so.

The incisors ripped through flesh and bone. His body was twisted and bent into shapes they weren't meant to be twisted and bent into.

But Kikko felt nothing. And he didn't care.

He only had one regret. *Should've killed Derek first. That was short-sighted. I'll know better next time.*

His last thought was, *Goodbye, Naru.*

The news that Colonel Wayne had just received from Lieutenant Castro in the AWAC plane had not made him happy. They hadn't picked anything up out on the open sea. At last report, they were heading in closer to Malau, where Wayne had been hoping they wouldn't need to go. *I do not want that thing crawling up my ass.*

The news that he received a few minutes after that from Corporal Macdonald back at MacArthur made him much happier. When Bateman had made his little announcement about Fox News, Wayne thought he was going to be up to his eyeballs in press. Bad enough that two journalists were missing and presumed dead and another injured—*paparazzi*, true, but still photojournalists—the last thing he needed was a bunch of microphone jockeys second-guessing him on-site.

Thankfully, that wouldn't happen.

Wayne found Bateman dictating notes into a tape recorder on the beach. "Good news," Wayne said.

Bateman stopped the recorder and said, "Oh?"

"Brigadier General Cox is ordering the media restricted to Kalor. I'm making you a one-man press pool. You'll be giving them official releases from here by phone. Talk to Sergeant Morwood about getting a cell phone."

"Uh, okay." Bateman looked stunned.

Wayne slapped the reporter on the shoulder.

"Welcome to the big leagues, kid," he said, and walked off.

As Bateman ran over to find Morwood, Ellway and Hale approached.

"Topex has been recalibrated," Hale said, answering Wayne's question before he had the chance to ask it. "If they get anything, they'll contact your Lieutenant Castro for confirmation—and he'll also relay it to us."

Wayne nodded. "Good work." He turned to Ellway. "Now what do we do when we find the thing?"

Before Ellway could answer, Wayne's radio squawked. "Malau, this is Lieutenant Castro."

Putting the radio to his lips, he said, "This is Wayne—go, Lieutenant."

"Colonel Wayne, we're picking something up, about sixty feet long, just off the coast of Malau. Something's travelling alongside it—about nine feet long."

Wayne sighed. *Well, that certainly kills two lizards with one stone.* "Thank you, Lieutenant. Keep tracking. Out." He lowered the radio and turned to the two scientists. "Gentlemen, I need to hear your plan *now*."

TWELVE

Before he and Hale outlined their plan to Colonel Wayne, Jack had wanted to find President Moki. Wayne had no problem with that, and indeed seemed chagrined that he hadn't thought of putting the president in the loop in the first place.

They found him at his restaurant, locking it up. The structure had managed to remain undamaged in the mother creature's initial stroll through town, for which Jack was grateful. "All secure, Mr. President?"

Moki turned to the three new arrivals and nodded. "Indeed."

"I'm glad the place made it through okay," Jack said. "After all, Malau's going to become a hot-ticket tourist trap. Wouldn't want to deprive people of the island's best restaurant."

For the first time since meeting him, Manny Moki allowed himself a big smile. "I appreciate your optimism, Jack. I hope it is not misplaced."

Hale said, "That's kinda why we're here."

"Our brain trust claims to have a plan," Wayne said. "So let's hear it."

They started walking back toward Wayne's command post on the beach. "Okay, we're going to need a boat, a good-sized sound system, some recording equipment, and explosives."

Wayne blinked. "Explosives? We talking dynamite, tactical nukes, what?"

"Lower end of the scale," Hale said with a smile.

"Basically," Jack said, "we need to lure Dad and Junior by using two different sets of sounds: the baby creature's voice to attract it to the boat—"

"—and ultra-high-frequency to keep it from getting dangerously close," Hale finished.

"I've used high-frequency sounds before, to protect whales by keeping them out of certain areas." That had been on the Hawaii trip—his and Brandon's first after Diane's death. It was actually one of the more productive journeys they'd taken. There were few enough humpback whales left in the world, and there would have been two fewer but for Jack's efforts on that trip.

Hale picked up the ball again: "We'll return the creatures to their home in the Iozima Ridge."

"And to keep them from coming back," Jack said, "we'll cut off their access to the fault line by setting off explosive charges—that's where the explosives come in."

"They'll implode the trench, filling it in."

Wayne and Moki had both been looking at Jack and Hale throughout their litany with poker faces. After they finished, there was a long pause. Then Wayne smiled a small smile. *Geez*, Jack thought, *I figured I'd go my entire life without seeing either of these guys smile, and now I've seen both do it inside of five minutes. Go figure.*

"Well, you guys sure don't think small," Wayne said.

The colonel's radio had been squawking with various

conversations throughout, but Jack had tuned them out. One, however, caught his attention. "Malau base, this is MacArthur for Colonel Wayne."

"Excuse me a minute," Wayne said, unhooking the radio and walking off to the side to have his conversation in privacy.

"Have you acquired a boat for this mission?" Moki asked.

Jack shook his head. "Not yet." Hale could have gotten a boat from his institute, of course, but they didn't want to risk bringing it here with all the giant lizard activity in the area—not to mention the military presence. No, they were better off using a boat already on Malau, but the only thing the pair of them had was the *Scorpion Fish*, which wasn't practical for the purpose.

"Well, now you have," Moki said. "You will take mine."

Jack smiled. That solved several problems right there. When they had had dinner several lifetimes ago, the president had mentioned that he owned a good-sized boat—not quite a yacht, but more than a simple motorboat. "That's very generous, sir," he said. "We can use my camcorder to record the baby's voice. Now if Colonel Wayne will just give us what we need, we'll be more or less set."

Just then, Wayne came back to rejoin the group. He had his "business face" back on, which didn't surprise Jack. "You wanted to hear a plan, Colonel. That's the plan. What we need from you is help with the detonation."

Wayne hesitated only for half a second, but it was enough. *Something's wrong*, Jack thought. He'd only known the colonel a short time, but in that time he had never hesitated before speaking.

"This is no longer my operation. The 31st MEU is on its way from Okinawa. They'll be here in twenty-four hours."

Jack opened his mouth, closed it, opened it again. He was stunned. "With—with what orders?"

"General Cox will be calling the shots from now on. I have no more power in this."

"That's it? You just walk away? It's, 'So long guys, go to hell'?"

"I have my orders," Wayne said tersely.

So much for Wayne not following the stereotype of the hidebound military nitwit, Jack thought with disappointment. "Fine," he said, "we'll do it without you." He turned to Hale. "We can talk to the chief—he can probably get us a line on some explosives. Hell, whoever blew up that truck to distract the two guards on the nine-footer has to have gotten that explosive from *somewhere*."

"It's a possiblity, yeah," Hale agreed.

The president turned on Wayne. "Do you force us to defy your orders, Colonel?"

Jack could have cheered. This island was still Manny Moki's turf. Jack wasn't sure how, exactly, jurisdiction would work in this case, but from what Paul had told him days before, the U.S. military were there as a courtesy to an independent nation. And that independent nation had just taken a stand in Jack and Hale's favor.

After another uncomfortable silence, Wayne raised his radio to his lips. "Master Sergeants Field and Hughes, report to command. Say again—Field and Hughes, report to command, immediately. Out."

I don't believe this. "Putting us under house arrest?" Jack said, both outraged and aghast.

"They're demolition experts," Wayne said.

Jack blinked in surprise.

"You see," Wayne continued, "I was just thinking about the message that my corporal passed on. What it said was that General Cox would take over upon the arrival of the 31st." He looked around. "They ain't here yet. So I'm still in charge for the time being, and I say that when Field and Hughes report to you, give them the coordinates. They'll set the charges and be ready when you get the creatures back home."

Jack shook his head. *I've been making a career out of misjudging people since I got here*, he thought. *Gotta watch that.* He reached out his hand and said, "Thank you, Colonel."

Wayne accepted the handshake and said, "Good luck." Then he walked off.

Jack looked at Moki, then at Hale. "Well, we've got our work cut out for us."

"And then some," Hale said.

"Come," Moki said, "I will take you to the boat."

Paul Bateman studied himself in the mirror. *This is stupid*, he thought, looking at his neatly combed hair and his tucked-in shirt. Not since Mak's daughter's christening had he gone to the trouble to seriously groom himself beyond what was necessary to politely interact with the rest of humanity.

Now, though, he'd been upgraded. *From rinky-dink weekly newspaper on a backwater island to sole press link to the biggest story of the year. Not bad for a California surfer dude.*

The neatening up really hadn't been necessary. After all, he was communicating by cell phone. He could be in his bathrobe, and no one would be the wiser. But it was the principle of the thing.

He had already made one introductory call to the press room on Kalor. He imagined something out of *His Girl Friday*, with a bunch of guys in fedoras leaping onto old hook-and-mouthpiece phones and reading notes copied onto spiral notebooks. In reality, they were probably all carrying cell phones, had made their notes on laptops, and weren't wearing hats of any kind, but Paul still liked the image.

The call had informed him that, as he himself had predicted, CNN was only the beginning. Every major wire service, newspaper, TV network, and online news provider had a representative on Kalor wanting to know what was happening. He had told them that they would have an official press release inside an hour.

Now an hour later, Paul was ready to make the call. He'd written a release, run it by Sergeant Greene, to whom Wayne had delegated the task of approving all releases, and was now ready to pass it on to the rest of the world.

He had no idea how the information was going to be transferred. There was a woman named Carla something who ran the press room on Kalor, who would no doubt pass the info on and relay any questions to Paul. Paul also intended to e-mail the release to a variety of sources—but first, the phone call.

"Hello?" came Carla's voice before the first ring ended.

"Hi, Carla, this is Paul Bateman from the *Malau Weekly News*. I have a release for the press corps."

"About time," she muttered.

"At thirteen hundred hours yesterday, the 43rd Marine Expeditionary Unit from the island of Kalor arrived on Malau under the command of Colonel J. Christopher Wayne." Idly, Paul wondered what the "J" stood for. *Wonder if it stands for John*, he thought, then decided that would just be too corny. "They came in response to a direct request from Malau President Manuel Z. Moki to the threat of a previously unknown and uncatalogued reptile." Paul had originally written this in the plural, but Sergeant Greene had insisted on keeping it singular, on the theory that one giant lizard was spooky enough, thanks. "This reptile is believed to be responsible for three unexplained deaths on Malau over the last week, as well as an attack on three photojournalists. Two of those journalists—Marcello Silverio and John Hawkins—are missing, with a third—Pierce Askegren—having been evacuated from the Malau Clinic to Kalor General Hospital this morning with several injuries. The 43rd expects to have the situation under control within the next twenty-four hours, at which point they will have the reptile in captivity." He took a breath. "That's it."

"I assume two of the people who died are Marina Greenberg and Carol Franz," Carla said. Paul remembered that that story had made the wire services. "Who was the third?"

"A Malauan named Dak Malano."

"We understand that the 31st MEU from Okinawa is on its way to take over the operation. If the situation is under control, why is the larger force needed?"

That one caught Paul off guard. Greene had told him to answer all questions he didn't know the answer to with a "no comment," which is what he did in this case.

"What about the rumor that President Moki has been placed under house arrest for questioning the authority of the U.S. military forces?"

Where do they come up with these things? "That is most definitely not true. Colonel Wayne and President Moki get along just fine, and in fact Manny was the one who called in the 43rd in the first place."

"We've gotten reports of a nine-foot-long creature, another of a forty-foot one, and yet another of a two-hundred-foot one. Which is the right size?"

Paul chose his words carefully. "A nine-foot reptile has been sighted on Malau, and the military's intention is to capture the creature within the next twenty-four hours."

"So what about this two-hundred-foot-long one?"

Smiling, Paul said, "There is no reptile of that size that I'm aware of."

"Okay. Hang on, I think I've got a couple more questions."

"Sorry," Paul said, leaping at the opportunity, "but I've got to go. I'll call back in an hour or two. Or three."

"But—"

He pressed the END button on the cell phone before Carla could protest further.

Whew. Paul wiped the sweat from his brow. *I do not want to go through that again. Being a one-man press corps isn't all it's cracked up to be.*

At least, not under military jurisdiction. He supposed he could have just ignored Greene and gone ahead and told the whole truth, but if he did that, his status would go quickly from one-man press corps to latest guy on the evac plane.

He got up from his desk and peered out the window. He saw Jack, Doc Hale, and Manny all standing outside talking. *Well, let's see what our resident mad scientists have come up with.*

As he went outside, Jack said, "Got a breaking story for you, Paul. Feel like coming along?"

"Sure," he said gleefully. *I'll take being out reporting over answering awkward questions any day.*

"Great," Jack said. "Bring a lifejacket."

Paul frowned. "Excuse me?"

Jack laughed. "C'mon, I'll explain on the way."

They started to walk toward the pier, but were intercepted by Joe Movita. "We just found a body," he said to Manny without preamble.

"My God," said Manny, crestfallen. "Whose?"

"Kikko. At least, what was left of his body. He'd been torn to pieces."

Paul shuddered. "So the nine-footer's still on the island."

"Or was," Hale said. "The AWAC tracked it with the big 'un out on the ocean."

Joe was shaking his head, however. "Whatever did this wasn't the same thing that attacked Jimmy—the pattern of wounding is similar, but whatever did this is a good deal larger."

"The father lizard?" Jack said.

"That'd be my guess, yeah. The funny thing is, Kikko had a harpoon gun and a rope with him."

Manny shook his head. "Thank you for this information, Chief."

Joe nodded, and went off in the direction of the clinic.

"What the hell was he doing with a harpoon gun?" Paul asked.

Jack shrugged. "We can worry about that later. C'mon, let me tell you our cunning plan."

As they walked toward the pier, Jack did so, and Paul had to admit to being impressed with either their ambition or their stupidity.

"Yowza," he said when they were finished. He turned to Hale. "Y'know, we're gonna have to *completely* redo your interview at this point."

Hale laughed. "Prob'ly, yeah. One thing we still need are the speakers. I already talked to the blokes in the dive shop about some waterproof housing for 'em, and we've got recording equipment and the ultra-high-frequency broadcaster, but we're gonna need some serious speakers to attract these guys' attention."

"Not *too* serious," Jack said. "Remember, sound travels very efficiently underwater."

Paul nodded. "Either way, I think we should be able to prevail upon some local help—assuming they haven't been evacuated." He grinned. "In fact, if they *have* been evacuated, it'll be a lot easier to borrow it."

"Borrow it," Jack said dubiously, then looked at Hale. "Are all reporters this larcenous?"

"Nah," Hale said, "they're usually worse."

"Sir, you impugn me," Paul said with mock indignance. "In any case, Dak was part of a band called Friends Anemones. They've got a huge sound system in a garage on the outskirts of town."

"As it happens," Manny said, "the members of our friend Dak's group have already been evacuated—without their equipment, which would have put them over the weight limit. As I recall, Maru was rather vocal in his displeasure with this turn of events. However, their instruments and sound system are, in fact, being stored at the airfield."

"Beauty," Hale said. "Paul, whyn't you and I go fetch that stuff?"

"Sounds like a plan," Paul said.

Manny said, "Meanwhile, Jack, I will show you to my boat."

"Actually," Jack said, looking as if he'd just remembered something, "I'll meet you there. I need to get back to the hotel and—well, see to the baby. And, ah, and to Brandon."

Paul understood immediately. They needed the little lizard for their cockamamie plan to work. *And Jack wants Brandon to get on the next plane outta here.*

"Of course," Manny said, "I will meet you there."

Hale gestured in the general direction of the airfield. "After you, mate."

Paul nodded and went with the geologist.

For the third time in fifteen minutes, Jack had to explain his and Hale's plan—this time to Brandon, whom he had found on the lawn behind the Ritz, still frolicking with Casey. He had almost not wanted to disturb the idyllic scene, but he had to. First, though, he had to bring Brandon up to speed—especially since part of the plan was to separate Brandon from his new pet.

"I know you're gonna miss him," Jack said quickly, before Brandon had a chance to object to losing Casey so soon after finding him, "but we're doing the right thing, Brandon. We're doing what's right for him."

Jack steeled himself for the expected complaints, the implorations to let Casey stay with Brandon forever.

As usual for Jack since arriving on this island, he got the exact opposite reaction he expected.

"I know, Dad. I knew you'd figure out how to save him."

When will I learn to stop underestimating my kid? Jack thought with a smile.

Then Brandon added, "Let me go with you."

Sighing, Jack said, "I can't do that." He had expected this reaction, as well, and was rather dismayed to find that this one was spot-on.

"He'll freak without me. *Please*, Dad."

"I can't, Brandon," Jack said firmly, even though Brandon did have a point. Casey and Brandon had developed a bond, and having that bond around would have been useful. But the plan involved close proximity to a pair of creatures who were, between them and the dead female, responsible for over half a dozen deaths already—not to mention all the high explosives. He couldn't expose Brandon to that.

Brandon looked down, unhappy. He crouched back onto the grass so he could cradle Casey in his arms.

Great. Here we go again. It's my own damn fault for taking him all over the place. To him, this probably doesn't seem any more dangerous than half the things we've done the last year. Maybe I should've just stayed home, gone back to teaching again.

He sighed. *Right, and lived in that house some more with all its reminders of Diane.*

Shaking his head, he looked up to see Alyson Hart approaching.

"Hi," she said with that amazing smile of hers. "Paul told me what you're doing. I thought you might want me to look after Brandon—make sure he's evacuated okay."

"I'd really appreciate that," Jack said gratefully. In fact, he was almost fawning in his gratitude, and when he realized how much so, he cursed himself. *That's right, Jack, another problem successfully avoided by the usual Ellway method: running away.*

"Well," Alyson said, "see you on Kalor tonight."

"Yeah," he said, forcing himself to return her smile—which wasn't that hard, really. Alyson made him feel very much at ease. "See you on Kalor."

Oh, what the hell. He leaned forward and gave her a brief hug. Then he joined Brandon in his crouch on the lawn.

Reaching for Casey, he said, "I guess we'd better get him used to me holding him."

At first, Brandon seemed reluctant to part with the little animal, but after a second he let go of him. Jack didn't pick him up at first, but gently petted Casey, giving him a chance to get used to Jack.

He glanced over at Brandon to see a look of great sadness on his son's face. *Damn—this is harder for him than I thought. Probably harder than* he *thought. It's easy enough to tell me that I'm doing the right thing, but to actually have to give Casey up is a whole other thing.* "Don't worry, Brandon," he said, trying to be reassuring, "I'll get him home safely."

Brandon's response was so quiet Jack barely heard it. "He doesn't have a mother at home."

"But he's got a dad," Jack said, trying not to read too much into that statement. "He's gonna be reunited with his dad."

"But what if he isn't?" Brandon cried, and this time he was quite loud. "What if something happens to his dad?"

"Nothing's gonna happen to his da—" Jack started, but Brandon interrupted.

"The dad could die!" Brandon cried, throwing his arms up and down. "And then he'll be an *orphan*!"

"I'm gonna do everything I can to make sure—"

This time it was Alyson who interrupted. "Jack, he's not talking about the creatures."

Jack shot her a look, then looked back down at Brandon.

When Diane died, Brandon hadn't broken down. Tears flowed, of course, both the morning it happened and during the funeral—it was impossible for them not to—but he never really *cried*. Or if he did, it wasn't in Jack's presence. At the time, Jack thought he was just trying to be strong. And perhaps he was.

But whatever strength he had marshaled had apparently now evaporated. Tears streaked down Brandon's face from red eyes as he wailed, "I don't want you to die! I don't have anybody but you!"

Jack pulled his son to him and hugged him hard. "Aw, Brandon," he muttered, and kissed him on the head.

I can't just leave him like this.

A year ago, his brother Stephen had offered to take Brandon in when the go-ahead for the Hawaii trip came through. Jack had seriously considered the offer, then—but ultimately decided against it. Brandon had always come with him and Diane on their jaunts to various parts of the world—"making the world safe for marine biology," as Diane had joked—and to have gone without him then would have been foolish on two fronts. To in essence abandon Brandon so shortly after his mother had, through death, done likewise would have been cruel. And besides, without Diane, he needed Brandon's help.

"Brandon, you and me—we're all we've got."

"Brandon—the past year, all the running around we've done...has it been okay for you?"

"When you lose someone—someone who took care of you—it helps if someone's there to take over. Someone else who can love you and protect you."

Jack broke the embrace and looked down at his son, who had stopped crying, though his eyes were still red. *I can't go off on my own now any more than I could a year ago.*

"Come," he said. "I won't leave you alone."

Brandon sniffed. "Uh, Dad? How soon is the boat gonna leave?"

"Probably twenty minutes to half an hour. It kinda depends on how soon those two sergeants can set up the explosives and how long it takes to set the speakers up. Why?"

Now Brandon looked sheepish. "Well, uh, can we do any of that after the boat leaves?"

"I guess so," he said, wondering where Brandon was going with this. *Admittedly, I'd rather do this sooner than later, but I'd rather do it right than sooner.* "Why, Brandon?"

"Well, see," he said hesitantly, "Derek thinks I'm helping him kidnap the baby."

"What?" On the one hand, Jack couldn't believe it. On the other hand, he had no trouble believing it—there was very little at this point that he didn't believe Derek Lawson to be capable of.

"I sent him on a wild goose chase, but he's gonna figure it out. I told him I'd meet him at his boat in an hour." Brandon looked at his watch. "That was about forty minutes ago. We were gonna take his boat to Kalor. He said that you couldn't protect Casey from being dissected by scientists. But I knew you'd figure out a way to keep him safe."

Jack was warmed by his son's vote of confidence, even after all this.

"And," Brandon continued, "even if you couldn't, I wasn't gonna leave Casey with *that* jerk."

Laughing, Jack tousled his hair—in, he realized belatedly, the same manner that Derek did at Manny's their first day here. Brandon, however, smiled, so he obviously didn't mind.

He turned to Alyson. "I guess we'll both be going, then."

"Yeah," she said, smiling. "So much for my brilliant plan. They evac'd all my patients, so I figured this was a good way to take care of *someone*. Physician's instincts, y'know?"

Again, Jack laughed. "Right. Well, I'm sure I'll see you later."

She rubbed her hands for no obvious reason, and said, "Yeah. On Kalor."

"Right," Jack said.

And with that, she walked off.

Part of Jack wondered if there was more to it than "physician's instincts." Another part of him pointed out that Alyson lived on Malau and wasn't likely to leave, while Jack lived in San Diego.

Of course, it might not be a bad idea to get a fresh start....

Shaking his head, he thought, *I'll worry about that later. Right now, we have work to do.*

He led Brandon and Casey toward the pier.

THIRTEEN

Jack and Brandon arrived at the pier to see President Moki, Doctor Hale, Paul, and two Marine sergeants—he assumed these latter two were Field and Hughes, Wayne's demolition experts. Hale and Paul had already put on lifejackets, and were lugging various bits of equipment onto Moki's boat.

"Ah, Jack," Hale said upon sighting him. "These two blokes are Mike Field and Bernie Hughes. They'll be handlin' the explosives."

"Jack Ellway," he said, shaking each sergeant's hand in turn.

Field said, "Colonel Wayne said that we were to be at your disposal, sir."

Jack nodded and looked at Hale. "You have the map?"

"Yeah," Hale said. "Think you can handle the rest'a this, mate?" he asked Paul.

"I'll muddle through, yeah," Paul said as he hauled a large speaker encased in plastic onto the deck.

Hale smiled and rummaged through some papers before liberating the topographical map. "We're gonna be leadin' the creatures to their homes in the Iozima Ridge. What we're gonna need you lot to do is—"

"Blow it up at the fault line, imploding the ridge?" Field ventured.

"Uh, right," Hale said, looking as nonplussed as Jack felt. "How'd you know about the fault?"

"We're Marines, sir. It's our job to know."

Jack hid a smile. Hale just grunted. "Right," the latter said. "The coordinates—"

"We know where the fault line is, sir. With your permission, we need to gather up the semtex—we can be airborne in five."

"That's great," Jack said quickly, not giving Hale a chance to respond. "Stay in touch via radio—we'll let you know when we need you to make things go boom."

Hughes actually smiled at that. "Going boom is our specialty, sir." And with that, the pair of them moved off.

"Bloody showoffs," Hale muttered.

"You're just cranky 'cause you didn't get a chance to give a lecture," Jack said, slapping Hale on the back.

Moki stepped forward. "I too must depart. Best of luck to all of you." The president shook each of their hands in turn, even Brandon's, and he gave Casey a little pat on the head.

"We won't let you down, sir," Jack said.

"I'm sure you won't," the president said with a small smile, and then he, too, left.

Sighing, Jack turned to the others. "C'mon, let's get this show on the road."

Derek Lawson was furious.

The damn kid was late, and Kikko had disappeared. *And now they're evacuating the bleedin' island, and sooner or later they're gonna make me leave. Well, that ain't happenin' without* one *of those beasts.*

Then he heard the sound of a motor approaching and heading eastward. *What the hell?*

He saw the familiar sight of Manny's boat sailing out into the open sea at a rather brisk clip. Standing on its deck were Ellway, Bateman, Hale—

—and Ellway's kid, the little monkey cradled in his arms.

I don't bloody believe this. That little bastard!

Derek punched the wall to the bridge in frustration. *The little twerp double-crossed me!*

He went over to the side to untether the boat. As he did so, Chief Movita approached. "Hello there, Derek."

"If you're lookin' for a ride off the island, mate, tough luck. I'm evacuatin' on my own, soon's I can find Kikko." That was a lie, both that he was evacuating and that he was waiting for Kikko, but Joe didn't need to know the truth.

"I'm afraid I can't let you do that, Derek. See, I've got bad news and bad news."

As he tossed the ropes onto the boat, freeing it from the dock, Derek said, "Joe, I ain't in the mood—"

"The bad news," Joe continued, oblivious to Derek's desire to get moving so he could catch up to Manny's boat and claim his property, "is that we found Kikko's body."

That brought Derek up short. "What?"

"He was ripped to pieces. The current popular theory is that there's another big monster out there."

Damn, Derek thought. *Poor bloke. I should've gone with him. Dammit.*

"As for the other bad news—well, it's been a little crazy around here, but I did finally get a chance to dust the nine-footer's cage and chain for fingerprints. Imagine my surprise to find that two of the matches were for Kikko and Naru."

Without missing a beat, Derek said, "My God, you think they freed the beast?"

"Don't play dumb with me, Derek. Those two don't go to the bathroom without your prior permission. You were trying to steal the thing and screwed it up. I bet that's how Naru *really* got hurt, too." Joe took a pair of handcuffs out. "Either way, you're under ar—"

Joe was unable to finish the sentence, occupied as he was with falling over backward from Derek's punch to his face. Trying to shake the pain of the impact free from his hand, Derek ran up to the bridge and started the motor.

Goddammit, the whole bloody thing's gone to hell.

The sound of a bullet ricocheting off the bow forced him to turn around. He saw Joe firing on the boat.

Keeping his head down, Derek steered the boat in the same direction as Manny's boat had gone. After a moment, when he was out of Joe's firing range, he set his trawler right in the other boat's wake.

Only one thing for it, he thought, eyeing the remaining harpoon gun. *Gotta get that little monkey away from Ellway and his brat.*

Jack nervously surveyed the ocean. Intellectually, he knew that the two creatures would remain below the surface. They could move more efficiently through the water if they stayed immersed. The only reason to go above water was to obtain food—and right now, they were more likely to find food underwater.

But he kept looking anyhow.

Lieutenant Castro had radioed the position of the two reptiles some fifteen minutes previous. Paul—who had been given piloting duties, amidst crowing over getting to drive the presidential yacht—had changed course so that they would be in front of the pair. Jack had then hooked up the camcorder—with which Brandon had recorded the baby's voice shortly after they shoved off—to one speaker, while Hale had done the same with the other speaker and the ultra-high-frequency broadcaster.

"We're in position," Paul said from the bridge.

"Right," Jack said, and looked at Hale. "Ready to lower the booms?"

Hale grinned at the figure of speech. "I thought those two smartass sergeants were handlin' that."

"Very funny. Let's do it."

"How far down do we want the high-frequency speaker?" Hale asked as he hefted it over the rail. They had had to attach weights to either side of the speaker so it wouldn't float.

"About twenty feet," Jack said.

"Right." Hale started lowering it into the water via the wire that connected it to the broadcaster.

Jack then lowered the other speaker, which wasn't weighted, down to the water. It trailed obediently behind the boat like a trained water skier.

"Okay," he said, "let's do a sound check."

Hale flipped two switches on the broadcaster, and the needle on one display swung all the way around to the other side. "The high-frequency's working," he said.

"Or at least the needle is," Jack said with a smile. Then he noticed that Casey was tense in Brandon's arms on the deck. He pointed at the baby. "Actually, based on that, it's working. As long as it stays underwater and he's above water, it won't repulse him the way it should for the others, though." He said that last primarily for Brandon's benefit, as the creature's sudden tension made the boy apprehensive.

Jack walked over to the camcorder and hit the PLAY button. "Camcorder's on."

Suddenly, the sound of Casey's voice could be heard

at a greatly amplified volume behind the boat. The baby himself looked around in confusion at hearing his own voice while not actually using it. Brandon fed him a cheese puff to calm him down as Jack pressed the STOP button.

"Let's check the sonar," he said to Hale. "We can get an exact position."

They walked over to the sonar, which had, along with the broadcaster, come from Hale's bungalow. The nine-footer was too small to register, but a sixty-foot-long reptile most assuredly wasn't. It was moving alongside the boat. According to the sonar display, a green screen with tiny green pixels of varying intensity indicating mass picked up in the water, it was a bit over nine hundred meters away and thirty meters down. *Good, safe distance*, Jack thought.

Brandon stood behind Jack and pointed at the sonar display while looking at Casey. "That's your dad," he said. Jack smiled, and wondered if the creature truly understood that that green blob on the screen actually represented his father.

He moved over to the camcorder and once again hit PLAY. Again, the sounds of Casey's voice were heard from the stern.

From the sonar, Hale said, "It's turned and is moving toward us. It must be hearin' the sound."

"What should I do?" Paul called from behind the wheel.

"You're doing it," Jack said. "Just maintain a steady course."

"Steady. Right."

Jack smiled and moved over to the broadcaster. This was the tricky part. Casey's voice would lure it closer, but if it got too close, the president's boat would be returning to Malau as splinters. His hand hovering over the switch to turn the ultra-high-frequency noise on, he said to Hale, "Tell me when."

"Almost...almost...almost...*now*."

Jack flipped the switch.

In Brandon's arms, Casey twitched.

"Hell and damnation," Hale muttered, "it's still approaching, it—wait." He let out a breath. "It's eased off. The high-frequency's keepin' it back about forty-five meters."

Paul's sigh of relief at this news was audible on the deck.

Jack peered over Hale's shoulder at the display. "It's following us, though. Right where we want it."

"Oh, *damn*!" Hale cried out suddenly.

Panicking, Jack said, "What? What?" *Did the sonar go wonky? Did the high-frequency cop out?*

"No, nothing, mate, nothing. At least nothing for you to worry about. No, I just remembered that I never did my *Scientific American* column. I promised my editor I'd have it in by Friday. With all this hugger-mugger, I completely forgot about the blessed thing."

Jack couldn't help it. He laughed. "In the realm of great tragedies we've seen in the last week, that ranks pretty low."

"You only say that 'cause you've never met my editor. She'll be right browned off, I can tell you that."

"I can't see him." That was Brandon's voice. Jack turned to see him standing at the stern railing, peering over the side as Jack had been doing several minutes earlier. Casey stood on the deck bench and peered between the slats of the railing. Brandon looked down at the baby creature. "Can you see him?"

Smiling, Jack turned back around and put on the radio headset. "Sergeant Field, this is Ellway, do you read?"

"Loud and clear, Ellway," said Field's voice over the tinny speakers of the headset. "What's the word?"

"We're on course, heading toward the creatures' home. Time to set the depth charges."

"Roger that, Ellway." After a second: "Depth charges away." After several more seconds: "Congratulations, Mister Ellway, you are the proud father of a dead fault line."

"Thanks, Sergeant," Jack said with a smile. "Give my regards to Colonel Wayne. Ellway out." He removed the headset and looked at Hale. "Okay, that's the easy stuff out of the way."

Suddenly, a spark flashed in the corner of Jack's eye. He turned to look at the broadcaster in time to see several more sparks. "Oh, no," he muttered.

Hale ran over to the broadcaster and started making some adjustments, but it kept sparking. "Hell and damnation," he said, "it's the circuitry. The high-frequency is failing." Quickly but gingerly, Hale removed a panel from the broadcaster.

Reluctantly, knowing full well what he would see and hoping against hope that he wouldn't see it, Jack looked at the sonar display. "The creature's getting closer," he said anxiously. The sonar placed it at thirty meters and closing very quickly.

Jack turned to see that Brandon was still standing by the back rail with Casey.

Beyond Brandon, he could see that the water was churning to a degree much greater than could be accounted for by simply being in the boat's wake.

As Jack ran to grab Brandon, he could feel the boat speeding up. *Thank you, Paul*, he thought as he wrapped his arm around Brandon's waist and pulled him away. He wasn't sure how much good it would do—the creature was big enough that it probably didn't matter what part of the boat one was on if it chose to attack—but it was probably safer at the center of the boat than the edges.

Brandon broke free, and Jack was about to protest when he saw that his son was going back for Casey, who still stood peering between the slats of the railing.

"Just a loose wire!" Hale called out.

Jack ran over to the broadcaster just as Hale reconnected a wire, then replaced the panel and switched the ultra-high-frequency back on. Jack turned to the sonar display to see that the creature was moving farther back—or, rather, since they were still moving at a good clip, the creature had stopped moving forward. Then, after a moment, it continued at a safer distance, this time staying fifty-five meters back. *The sudden burst of sonics that close must've spooked it.*

"Well, *that* was fun," Jack muttered. He looked up to the bridge. "You okay up there, Paul?"

"Oh yeah, just peachy," Paul said, sounding breathless. "I'll be fine the minute my heart restarts. Let's not do that again real soon, huh?"

"I'll do my best, mate," Hale said.

"Dad," Brandon said.

Jack looked at his son, and saw that he was gazing out onto the water behind them. Following his gaze, Jack saw a trawler making a beeline for their boat and gaining as fast as the reptile had done minutes earlier.

"What the hell?"

Then he recognized the man behind the wheel. *Derek. Jesus Christ, doesn't this guy ever quit?*

As he got closer, Derek pulled over to the port side of the president's boat. *Makes sense*, Jack thought, *that's the direction the current is going.*

Then he noticed something else: thanks to that selfsame current, the speakers had drifted in the same direction. And Derek was pulling his propellor-powered boat into a position that put those propellors dangerously close to the two speaker wires.

He cupped his hands over his mouth and yelled, "Stay back!"

Hale and Paul did likewise. "Back! Stay back!" "Derek, stay back!"

Still steering with one hand, Derek picked up what looked like a harpoon gun with the other. "Hand over the little one!" he cried out. "I want the little one!" The New Zealander's face had gone red, and his eyes looked wild. *I think our fisherman friend has lost it*, Jack thought, which might have given him some comfort—to Jack's way of thinking, fewer people deserved it more—but for the fact that he was dangerously close to destroying the only thing keeping them all from becoming giant-reptile food.

"Please, Derek, back off!" Jack cried.

"Shut your mouth! Just hand over the little one—*and* your rotten kid too, for security! I'll turn him loose when I'm safe!"

Like hell, Jack thought, and immediately guided Brandon below decks. To his credit, Brandon didn't even think of resisting, but grabbed Casey in his arms and went down the narrow staircase.

Paul shouted, "Derek, you moron, get out of here! The giant creature's right below us!"

Having safely stowed his son, Jack turned to look again at Derek's propellors—they were inches from the speaker wires. Then he looked at the sonar—the creature kept its distance at fifty-five meters, but that would change the minute those speakers stopped broadcasting.

Hale cried, "You're gonna kill us all, you maniac!"

"Don't think I wouldn't!" Derek yelled.

And then it happened: the propellor sliced right through the speaker wires. The wires emitted brief sparks that died in the water, and the speakers belonging to Dak's band floated off into the Pacific Ocean.

Hale said unnecessarily, "Jack, we've lost the wires."

Jack looked at the sonar. *Thirty meters and closing. We're toast.*

"I've got nothing to lose, mates," Derek was carrying on. "I'm not leaving without the creature and the boy!"

Twenty meters.

And then a massive head broke through the water.

For a moment, Jack Ellway couldn't move. He was in complete awe. The nine-footer had been magnificent in its "plumage" of horns; the mother magnificent in size and grandeur. This one combined both of those elements, and it was an amazing sight. Jack found himself hypnotized by the creature's majesty.

The hypnotism ended when it smashed Derek's boat.

Derek screamed. The creature trashed the rear of the trawler. Derek somehow had the presence of mind to leap off before the next swipe, which took the rest of it. Then he swam toward the president's boat.

"Y'know," Paul said, "we *could* leave him down there."

Jack had to admit to being tempted, but enough people had died already. "Grab my legs," he said to Hale as he got down onto his stomach. Once Hale did as he asked, he leaned out as far as he could and reached toward the water. "Grab my hand," he said to Derek.

To Jack's relief, Derek grabbed Jack's right wrist with his own right hand; Jack likewise grabbed Derek's wrist with his right hand, using his left to haul himself and the fisherman onto the boat.

To Jack's annoyance, Derek still held the harpoon gun in his left hand.

Jack reached for the harpoon gun, but Derek yanked it out of Jack's reach, then swung it around and hit Jack in the stomach with the handle.

Wheezing, Jack fell to his knees, grateful for the life-jacket he wore—it probably dulled the impact. Even with it, he had had the wind knocked out of him. Derek stumbled forward and tried to punch Jack in the face, but was thrown off balance by the rocking of the boat. The swing went over Jack's head.

Clutching his stomach with his left hand, Jack thrust a punch toward Derek's stomach, which doubled the fisherman over—but he still didn't relinquish the harpoon gun.

Jack made another lunge for the harpoon gun, but Derek once again hit Jack with the handle, this time in the upper thorax. Eye-tearing pain sliced through his chest. *Shit, I think he nailed a rib*, he thought as he lashed out with a backhanded punch to Derek's jaw.

And then Jack found himself propelled upward.

There is a moment that high-divers experience when they hit the apogee of their dive, that moment when they hang in the air, the force of their leap off the diving board finally starting to give way to gravity but not yet willing to relinquish its hold. For that one moment, one is free of any constraints, but free in the air.

Jack felt that moment seconds after punching Derek. In that split second before gravity reasserted itself and pulled him toward the harsh waters of the Pacific, he looked down and saw why he had been thrown skyward in the first place.

The creature, having completed its demolition of Derek's trawler, had apparently swum under the president's boat and come up through the bottom, splitting the vessel in half.

Somehow, Jack managed to convert his tumble downward into a passable dive. It took all his willpower to keep from inhaling sharply when the water collided with his bruised ribs. Within a few seconds, he was treading water, kept afloat by the graces of the lifejacket.

He looked around quickly, trying to take stock of the situation. He saw Hale swim over to where Casey was floundering in the water—the little guy seemed befuddled by this turn of events.

Oh God, Jack realized, *Casey's alone. Where's Brandon?*

Then he sighted his son, who was gazing at Hale with a look of relief on his face.

"Toss the gun away," came Paul's voice from behind

Jack. Maneuvering around in the water, Jack saw Paul holding a life preserver and speaking to Derek. Like the rest of them, Derek was treading water; unlike the rest of them, the New Zealander didn't have a lifejacket, and he looked like he wouldn't be able to keep the tread up much longer, especially since he *still* clutched the harpoon gun with his left hand like it was an extension of his arm.

"I mean it, Derek, toss the gun away," Paul repeated.

A snarl on his face, Derek did as he was told. The harpoon gun went flying off behind Derek, who then hungrily snatched at the proferred life preserver.

Okay, that accounts for all the humans, and for the baby. So what happened to Dad and Junior?

Suddenly, Brandon sank underwater.

It happened so fast, Jack almost didn't see Brandon actually go down. One minute he was dog-paddling over toward Hale and Casey, the next he was gone.

"Brandon!" he shouted.

When his son didn't resurface after a second had passed, Jack gingerly removed his life jacket, took several quick breaths to super-oxygenate his blood, and then dove under the surface.

Jack had never been the greatest swimmer in the world. *Relentlessly competent* was how Diane had described his swimming ability when they were dating, and he hadn't improved much in the subsequent ten-plus years. Add to that the bruised ribs, and it was a struggle to move downward, much less find his son. He had to rely much more on his feet than his arms, as each movement of his right arm sent splinters of pain shooting through his chest.

Within a few seconds of agonizing swimming, he found Brandon, whose lifejacket had gotten caught on one of the stray ropes from one of the two mangled ships. *But the rope's taut*, Jack realized. *That doesn't make sense.*

He peered down—to see that the other end of the rope was wrapped around the tail of the nine-footer.

Kicking fiercely toward Brandon, Jack noticed that both the giant creature and the nine-footer were swimming downward. *I guess they've given up on us. But why have they—?*

Then he remembered: *The Iozima Ridge. This is where they came from. I guess they've decided that life outside the nest is more trouble than it's worth. Nice to see my instinct was right.*

Unfortunately, their homesickness was threatening Brandon's life.

Ignoring the pain, he pushed ever downward, finally managing to snag Brandon. As he undid the boy's life-jacket, dark spots started to form in front of his eyes. His right arm felt sluggish as he wrapped it around his now-free son. A lecture from his scuba diving certification course came back to him: "It's not the oxygen deprivation that gets you, that makes your vision cloudy, that gums up your reflexes; it's the carbon dioxide buildup. CO_2 is *not* your friend."

He kicked as hard as he could toward the surface, using his left arm to push downward in the hopes of propelling himself up as fast as possible, cradling Brandon in his right.

On the way up, the baby creature came swimming down.

For a brief instant, Brandon and Casey exchanged glances. Brandon reached out and touched Casey's face.

Then they continued on their way, each back homeward.

Jack spared the baby one final look down as they tried to get surfaceward. Casey swam as fast as he could, trying to rejoin his brother and father.

The instant his head broke through the surface, Jack took the longest, deepest breath he'd ever taken—then cried out in pain, as the sharp intake pained his bruised ribs. But he didn't care—he'd never enjoyed taking a breath so much in his life.

A plank from one of the boats floated nearby, and they both grabbed onto it.

Then they looked at each other.

Brandon fell into Jack's arms and hugged him tightly.

That hurt even more than the breath had, and Jack cared even less. Part of him hoped Brandon would never let go.

Clutching his son in his arms, Jack looked over at Hale, who was smiling. "Did you free the baby?" he asked.

Hale nodded. "Yeah, I figured the little bloke belonged with his family."

"I can't bloody believe you did that," Derek said, rubbing his jaw. "Don't you realize—"

Paul rolled his eyes. "Give it a *rest*, Derek."

Hale suddenly perked up. "What's that sound?"

"What sound?" Jack asked. Then he heard it: a motor. He turned to see a boat with the letters USMC stencilled on the side.

Standing at the prow was Colonel Wayne. To Jack's amazement, he was grinning ear to ear.

"Someone call a cab?"

EPILOGUE

"Derek Lawson, you are under arrest."

Those were the first words Joe Movita said when Derek Lawson set foot onto Malau from the Marine boat. He said them as he grabbed Derek's arms and yanked them—perhaps a bit too violently—behind his back and applied handcuffs to the fisherman's wrists.

"What're the charges?" Ellway asked as he followed Derek off the boat—though, Joe noticed, the marine biologist moved more gingerly.

"Assaulting a police officer," Joe said, pointing to his left eye, which had swollen half shut.

"Ooh, that doesn't look good," Ellway said, taking a closer look at the chief's face. Then he clutched his side. "And this doesn't feel good."

"I'd say you should see a doctor, but she left on the last 'copter."

Colonel Wayne stepped down and looked angrily at Joe. "And how come you weren't on that copter, Chief?"

"I had some unfinished business with Derek here. Besides, Malau is my home. I've lived here all my life, and I've been responsible for its well being for all of my adult life. Captain goes down with the sinking ship, y'know?"

Wayne shook his head. "Yeah, well, you're lucky."

"How's that?"

Derek finally spoke. "These bleedin' idiots led the creatures back to their homes."

"Sonar confirmed it," Wayne said. "Dad, Junior, and the baby all went deep into the ridge."

"I don't think we'll be seeing them again," Ellway said. "My guess is that Junior and the baby went exploring out of the fault line and found themselves on Malau. Mom came after them, and ran afoul of the human predator. Dad came to retrieve Mom's corpse and finish her job of bringing the kids home."

"Gotta admire family loyalty," Doctor Hale added.

Joe shook his head. He'd never even met his own father, yet it was out of a sense of loyalty to him that he took on the role of the island's protector—the same role his father had taken on when he challenged the Japanese overlords of Malau during the war. *Odd that giant reptiles would have the same kind of loyalty.*

He also thought about Jimmy, to whom he had made a promise. In a sense, it had been kept, though Joe wasn't sure that Jimmy would see it that way.

Well, it'll have to do, he decided as he led Derek off.

By morning, most of the inhabitants of Malau had returned. They had barely had time to settle on Kalor before they were called back. But in Colonel J. Christopher Wayne's considered opinion, the threat had passed, so it was safe.

Hot on the locals' heels were the media, all of whom wanted to know everything about the monsters that had terrorized the island. The lack of any video footage disappointed them, as did Wayne's monosyllabic replies to their endless questions—Wayne hated dealing with the press, and eventually he said that he'd only talk to Bateman. The *Malau Weekly News* editor had done well for himself, as his were the only pictures of the nine-footer, but not nearly as well as that *paparazzo—what was his name? Askegrit or something?*—whose photo of Big Mama Lizard had been snatched up by every news agency on the planet.

From this point on, Wayne thought, *it's just cleanup after a successful mission.*

I just hope General Cox sees it that way.

Cox arrived in a helicopter several hours ahead of schedule. His full complement of troops were still on a troop carrier plowing its way through the Pacific from Okinawa. A tall, imposing man with a shaved head who always wore mirrorshades and smoked Cuban cigars, he had known Christopher Wayne since they were both newly promoted sergeants at the latter stages of 'Nam.

As he set foot off the chopper and ran over, bent double to stay out of the wash of the blades, he cried out, "Chris, you mind telling me what the *hell* is going on here?"

Wayne saluted first, which Cox returned. "If the general would be more specific as to—"

"Oh, can the crap, Chris, I'm not in the mood," Cox said as he removed a Havana from his shirt pocket. "I tell you I'm takin' over, and your response is to blow up a damn *ridge*." He bit off one end of the cheroot. "You wanna explain that one?" he asked as he lit it.

"You told me that you would take over the mission upon your arrival, General. I took that to mean that I still retained command *until* your arrival. I was given a plan that stood a good chance of solving the crisis with less risk than an all-out assault."

"And you used civilians on a military operation," Cox said, a haze of cigar smoke now floating around his cue-ball–like head.

"The civilians came up with the plan, and they had the expertise. Plus, the plan was sanctioned by the local government, at whose behest we were here. This is Malauan soil, General, and—"

"Wait one fucking minute. You're telling me that you were whipped by the guy who runs the fucking *restaurant*?"

Wayne glared directly into the general's eyes—or, at least, where he imagined the general's eyes to be behind the mirrorshades. "No sir, I'm telling you that I decided to go with the plan sanctioned by the duly elected leader of this sovereign nation."

Cox took a long drag on the cigar, then blew out a chimney's worth of smoke. Wayne hated cigars even more than he hated the tropics, but this was his commanding officer....

"It's a good thing for you this worked, Chris."

"A good thing for all of us, sir. A frontal assault would've resulted in a lot of dead Marines, and might not have worked."

Cox shook his head. "Fine, whatever. I'll call off my guys." He took another drag on the cigar. "Jesus fucking Christ, it's hot. Where does a guy go to get a drink in this hellhole?"

Wayne smiled. "Follow me, sir," he said as he led the general toward Manny's.

Jack Ellway stared at the screen of Mulder, his laptop computer, presently serving its intended function by sitting in his lap. He had been in the Malau Clinic since his return, having had Brandon and Paul bandage him up. When Alyson returned from Kalor, she fretted over her lone patient—the rest had remained in Kalor's superior facilities—redoing the bandages "so you don't look like the Mummy's love slave," and ordered him to rest in bed for at least a day.

Brandon had fetched his laptop so he wouldn't go crazy.

"What the hell're you doing?" came the voice of Alyson Hart.

Jack turned and looked sheepishly at her. "Uh, playing Minesweeper?" he ventured lamely.

"Right. News flash, Jack," Alyson said with that amazing smile of hers, "when your doctor says, 'You need rest,' that doesn't mean, 'You should chart fish migration patterns,' or whatever it is you do on that silly machine."

"You should listen to her, Jack."

Jack peered past Alyson to see that Doctor Hale, Paul, and Brandon had come into the room behind her.

It was Hale who had spoken. "This sheila knows her business," he added.

"Sexist terms notwithstanding," Alyson said, folding over the monitor on the laptop, "you should be relaxing. That's why I've kept those press vultures out of here."

Looking at Paul, Jack said, "So why'd you let him in?"

Putting his hand to his chest in mock outrage, Paul said, "You wound me, sir. Besides, I invoked local privilege. But I had to promise all nine hundred reporters out there some kind of statement on how you're doing."

Shaking his head in amazement at his new celebrity status, Jack said, "Tell them I'm fine." Jack had given a statement to the press earlier, after which Alyson had forbidden any press to set foot across the clinic's verandah without a verifiable injury. When Jack had pointed out that some of them might injure themselves in order to get an interview with Jack, Alyson promised to make sure that whatever the injury was, it would get infected.

"Uh, Dad?" Brandon said. "Doctor Epstein called. She

wants to know where your first report is. We, uh—we've been here a week, y'know."

Jack chuckled. In all the excitement, he had forgotten about the reason he came to Malau in the first place: to chart the effects of the seismic activity on the local marine life. He was to spend six weeks here, e-mailing a report to his supervisor, Doctor Emily Epstein of UCSD's Biology Department, every week.

"Geez," Paul said, "doesn't she watch the news?"

"Actually, she doesn't," Jack said. "When someone asked her what she thought about the O.J. verdict, she thought they were talking about orange juice."

Brandon asked, "So, uh, what do I tell her?"

"Tell her to put Fox News on." He laughed. "Then tell her I'll call her tomorrow."

Brandon smiled. " 'Kay."

"So, uh," Paul started, "can you give me a little more? If I go back out there with just, 'He's fine,' I'll get lynched."

"Oh come on, Paul," Jack said with a grin, "you're a big-time reporter now. Embellish."

Paul rolled his eyes. "Please. After running the one-man weekly for all these years, I'm just not cut out for this big-time crap. I'm waiting for this fifteen minutes to be over, so I can have my life back."

"I would've thought this *would* be your life, Paul," Alyson said with, Jack noticed, not a little snideness.

Paul shrugged. "After I graduated Berkeley, that would've been true. Hell, I've already got six job offers that I would've gladly killed for five years ago—but they're all off Malau. And, to be honest, I love it here."

Alyson blinked. "You never struck me as the senti-mental type, Paul."

"I have depths you never bothered to plumb, Doctor," Paul said archly. "Besides, it's not all sentiment. For one thing, tourism'll probably shoot through the roof 'round here, which means I can raise my ad rates with a clear conscience and make a killing. Now if you'll excuse me, I have to go embellish."

With that, Paul left. Hale, on then other hand, moved closer to Jack's bed. "I'm afraid I've gotta get a move on as well, Jack. Need t'get back to the Institute—Board of Directors got all browned off 'cause I was takin' 'unnecessary risks,' and a load of other crap, so I gotta go an' soothe 'em."

"Will you be coming back?" Jack asked.

"That's the plan. Still gotta put those seismographs through their paces. 'Sides, this is still the best place for a good nap," he finished with a grin. Offering Jack his hand, he said, "Listen, Jack, when your six weeks're up, give me a ring. We can always use a good marine biologist."

Jack accepted the handshake. "I may just do that," he said, though he looked at Alyson as he said it.

With that, Hale left.

Alyson smiled. "Six weeks, huh?"

"Well, five now, unless I can convince Emily to let me make up the time I lost chasing giant reptiles."

Checking over Jack's dressing, Alyson said, "Well, good. That gives me at least five weeks to convince you to accept Hale's offer." Flashing Jack another one of her amazing smiles, she turned and left the room.

Well, that's certainly an incentive to stick around, he thought.

"Dad?" Brandon said hesitantly.

"Yeah?"

"Do you *want* to stay here?"

Jack frowned. "Well, if we did—would you mind?"

Quickly, Brandon shook his head. "No way. This place is great! I was worried *you* wouldn't wanna stay."

Smiling, Jack reached out to his son and pulled him into a gentle hug. "Yeah, well, maybe it's time we stopped living like gypsies and settled down again."

"Sounds good to me," Brandon said.

What a week, Jack thought. *First I find a new genus of reptile, then I bring the remnants of one family together, then I settle the remnants of my own.*

He thought about the creatures they had discovered, a new species created by humanity's folly. *I wonder if there are any more of them. If not, they're destined to die out—there are just three males left. That's a damned shame.*

Thinking about Alyson, he thought, *But then, I found someone else. Maybe the giant creature will, too. I think after all this, we all, human and reptile, deserve some happy endings.*